"I wonder what the real reason is...."

Grant's eyes roamed over Fern. "What's the real truth behind this dawn foray of yours—barefoot, becomingly loosened hair, careless nudity? You must have guessed I'd hear you and be tempted to reexplore the fascinations of a body I used to enjoy."

"You're saying I'd—I'd stoop to coaxing you into bed with me?" Fern exploded. "Why should I?"

"For petty satisfaction, perhaps. Perhaps as a crafty means to an end. But it's not on, my would-be Delilah. Lovely as you are, handy as you are, and reluctant as I am to turn you down, I will not share a romp in your bed. Come on—on your way. I need some sleep."

The cruel insults hurt, and Fern slapped his bronzed face—hard.

JANE ARBOR
is also the author of these
Harlequin Romances

Many of these titles are available at your local bookseller.

For a free catalog listing all titles currently available, send your name and address to:

HARLEQUIN READER SERVICE
1440 South Priest Drive, Tempe, AZ 85281
Canadian address: Stratford, Ontario N5A 6W2

The Price of Paradise

by

JANE ARBOR

Harlequin Books

TORONTO • NEW YORK • LOS ANGELES • LONDON
AMSTERDAM • PARIS • SYDNEY • HAMBURG
STOCKHOLM • ATHENS • TOKYO • MILAN

Original hardcover edition published in 1982
by Mills & Boon Limited

ISBN 0-373-02509-2

Harlequin Romance first edition November 1982

CHAPTER ONE

'*YOU can't mean that?*'

At the incredulous shake of Fern's head emphasising the question, the corn-coloured aureole of her hair lifted and swung, settling again, strand by wafted strand as she stared at her father, willing that he should not have been serious.

But seemingly he had been. Scarcely a muscle moved in Sir Manfred Stirling's handsome, goatee-bearded face as he confirmed, 'On the contrary, I meant just what I said,' adding, 'I didn't suppose you would be pleased.'

'*Pleased?*' Fern's echo was shrill with dismay. 'Just as well you didn't think I'd feel anything but mad, cheated, tricked, conned——!'

Sir Manfred cut in sternly, ' "Conned"—don't use such cheap jargon to me!'

She ignored him and raged on, 'Telling me you were bringing me with you on a holiday trip to an—an *Eden* of a tropical island; coaxing me into wanting to come, when I'd got everything going for me in London; promising we'd come by the Company yacht instead of flying! And then—now, in fact, now that we're here and within half an hour of docking, you admit that Grant is here too, that you've known all along he would be. You *planned* it. I bet you plotted it with him. He knows you've brought me with

5

you, and now you're both laughing. And if you don't call that a confidence trick, a little mean squalor of a trick, what is it? What do *you* call it? What does he?' she demanded, panting for breath.

There was a moment before her father replied. Then he said, 'Of course I planned it. How otherwise should we be here? And in the end, before we sailed, I don't remember that I still had to twist your arm. You're of age and a married woman——'

'I'm not any more!'

Sir Manfred shrugged. 'A personal quibble of no legal worth. But as I was saying, you could have refused to come. I didn't frogmarch you on board.'

'Because you'd managed to persuade me that Maracca was an experience I oughtn't to miss— exotic, rare, colourful, the lot. And I fell for it. But talk about sugar on the pill! When you and Grant hatched this plot to punish me and bring me to heel, you had it made when you sold me Maracca—you certainly did!'

For answer Sir Manfred looked out of the stateroom window and nodded. Reluctantly Fern's glance followed his to the sapphire-blue of lazy water lapping gently at white harbour walls and, farther down the coast, creaming at the edge of narrow ribbons of palm-fringed sands. Lift the eyes, and there were the green and colour-splashed levels and curves and heights of Maracca Island, one of the loveliest jewels of the Indian Ocean, east from the African mainland by a thousand miles. 'To anyone with all their senses alive,

I wouldn't have thought it needed much selling,' Sir Manfred mused aloud.

'That's what I'm saying,' his daughter snapped tartly. 'From what I can see, you didn't overpaint it. Nor the journey out, which has been fabulous. But that doesn't excuse you and Grant from making use of it all to lure me here, and then keeping your mean plot to yourselves until it was too late for me to back out.'

Sir Manfred dropped ice into a tumbler, poured whisky over it and took a sip. 'That was necessary,' he said. 'But mean plot or no, Grant hasn't been part of it, isn't still.'

Blankly, 'But you said he was here! You've been talking to the Opal office by radio-telephone on the way over,' Fern exclaimed.

'Not to Grant. To Austin Logan, the present manager whom we're moving sideways and demoting a bit when Grant moves in to handle the offshore developments in which Logan has no experience and Grant has.' Sir Manfred paused. 'Experience, I should add, which he has gained in various oil outposts about the world where you refused to accompany him, to the understandable ruin of your marriage.'

Fern winced at the stern note in her father's voice, but she sprang to her defence. 'He couldn't expect me to share the kind of awful quarters he often had to live in, in the outlandish places Opal sent him to,' she argued.

'You knew he was an oil executive on roving commission when you married him. If you'd loved him——'

'I did love him. I——' She checked, biting her

lip. 'Anyway, he knew how I wanted to stay in London where all my friends are, and I couldn't see why you couldn't switch him to a post in the London Opal office, and we would have taken a town house, or at worst lived, say somewhere like Richmond or the Heath.'

Sir Manfred sighed. 'My dear, if you didn't realise what you were taking on with Grant Wilder, it wasn't for want of telling. *I* told you; he must have done. But no! After one winter stint in Canada——'

Fern shuddered. 'Canada was *awful*!'

'And part of Grant's commitment to his job. But as I say, you became the poor little rich girl betrayed into gipsyhood against her will. And so you left Grant and came home to father, where, may I be forgiven, I've cosseted you ever since.'

'I didn't leave Grant,' she denied. 'He left me— to go off to the Gulf or some place East.'

Sir Manfred allowed, 'It's an academic point. You parted—leave it at that. But now—and none too soon, considering some of your reckless idiocies and the worthless crowd you've been running around with—I've decided you shall meet again at my arranging and on my responsibility alone.'

'You—you can't play God like that!' she defied.

'I don't aspire to. I'm merely father to a wilful daughter who's running away from being a woman; seeing it as his job to stop her running.' Sir Manfred drained his glass and came over to lay his arm across her shoulders. 'And so,' he continued, 'I've asked Grant to come aboard this evening for a drink.'

Fern jerked angrily away. 'Without telling him I'm here? What do you expect from that? That after one yelp of surprise he'll open his arms to me and I shall dash into them? Curtain. Soft music. Happy ending. After nearly three years apart? You must be joking!'

'After the way you treated Grant, he could well decide to slap your face, and I don't know that I'd blame him,' her father retorted. 'Meanwhile, I'd be a fool to expect miracles of your meeting, and having done my part by producing you, from there out you and Grant will be on your own with little or no help or hindrance from me.' He moved to her to drop a kiss upon her hair before going to the door. 'Even three wasted years aren't a lifetime of pigheaded folly. You could have plenty of time ahead. So keep your cool, Mrs Grant Wilder, and be at your prettiest tonight—hm?' he said as he went out.

Left alone, Fern leaned her face wearily against the sunwarmed glass of the window giving on to *Calypso*'s foredeck. Misjudged and near to tears of self-pity, she fought them back. She would *not* cry even in secret, for dread of the ordeal before her. She had done enough of that in the early days after Grant, having humiliated her to her depth, had flung away from her in revulsion and contempt and had left England on his latest mission without even calling up to say goodbye.

'*You parted—leave it at that.*' That was her father's impartial judgment of the breach

which had torn them apart. For that was all he
knew of it; all she had brought herself to tell
him—for her own pride's sake, for defence of
Grant, for the sake of a love which had never quite
flickered out and which for a long time she had
hoped might still burn for Grant. Even though,
against the background of that last violent scene
between them, it seemed unlikely he had ever
experienced a tolerant, understanding love for
her.

They had met at a party and had seemed electric for each other at once. They had met again,
almost always by his design or hers. Very soon
they had been talking their special lovers' shorthand and learning each other—or so Fern had
supposed—by heart.

She knew of his pride in having worked his way
up through Opal Oil from ground level, so to
speak. (Her father, now the Company's chief, had
done the same.) Grant had executive ambitions
and was in sight of them, and she had thought—
wrongly—that this would content him with a desk
job, ordering oil matters from there. Her wishful
thinking had ignored the fact that Sir Manfred,
who now did just that, was in his late sixties, while
Grant was 'outdoor' to his fingertips and only
thirty-three.

He had heard all about her background in
return. Nursery luxury, boarding school, riding
lessons, dancing tuition, finishing school in
Switzerland—all designed to make of her, at
nineteen or so, the matrix of almost every other
girl of her class and age. She had dabbled happily
at art classes, taught French, gratis, to her friends'

young children, and though her mother had died at about that time, leaving her as housekeeper for her father, the job had been much of a sinecure— the house had run itself in the hands of long-term, loyal staff.

So Fern had played the days and danced the nights away, secure in the belief that somewhere in the future—no hurry—there would be a husband and children and a house in at least a good suburb. Like Joan . . . and Anne . . . and Cecily, she would make a happy, successful, lasting marriage.

And then Grant had happened to her, exploding on her feminine sensuality like a meteor. Nothing like the magic he wrought for her, ever before. Nothing like the magic he had destroyed on that dreadful last night, ever again . . .

Sir Manfred had approved of Grant for her. 'There's granite-worth in the man,' had been his verdict on Grant, and so they had married, over-indulged nineteen to rugged, purposeful thirty-three. 'Just the right ages for a happy marriage,' the dowagers had cooed at the wedding, and had been just as ready to claim they had forecast doom when the marriage had split.

That scene . . . It had been the culmination of many small arguments and had finally erupted when Fern had told Grant that though she had borne months of Arctic cold in Canada for his sake, she had no intention of being roasted alive on the Persian Gulf. She had meant that half in joke, but he had taken her seriously.

'You married me, knowing what my job

entailed. You'll come where I have to go, or we'll call it a day,' he had told her.

Appalled by the threat, 'Do you mean you'd go without me?' she had faltered.

'If you refuse to go with me, have I any choice?' he had countered.

'Of course you have! We've been over all this before, and you know Father would make a place for you at Headquarters any time,' she claimed. 'You can't mean to make me a kind of grass widow only six months after marrying me!'

'And you can't make me a computer button pusher behind a desk! I married you to make you my wife—to be with and look after and love. Not any kind of widow—you'll only make yourself that if you walk out on me now.'

'I'm *not* walking out on you!'

'Let's not argue that toss. I'm walking out on *you*, if you can't be a wife to me and go with me where I have to. God, woman——' his anger had been patent then and she had been afraid—'if I'd thought that in marrying you I'd be allowed to take you to bed a few times and then be waved goodbye, I could have done as well with any woman, and no packdrill. I might even have taken one off the streets——'

For that she wanted to hit him, and would have done if he hadn't stayed her upraised hand, twisting her wrist painfully before flinging it from him.

'How dare you?' she demanded through her furious tears. 'How dare you compare me with—with——?'

'And what better or how different are you?'

'You—you should know.'

They had been in the bedroom of their furnished flat. Tardily getting ready for bed had always, until the happening she called simply 'Canada', been a sweet companionable time for them, a time for teasing play and talk. Sometimes when their desire had been impatient for each other, they had made love on the long divan at the foot of the bed, over which Grant had now stood, looking down at her, crouched against the cushions.

In a voice which sounded deep with menace he said, 'I thought I did. But how wrong can you get?'

'You weren't wrong! I'm not just any woman. I *am* different. I love you. I——'

'Love me!' he had jeered. 'My girl, all you know about love is just one thing, and for me that isn't enough. But if it's all you have to give, then I may as well avail myself, and thank you, ma'am, for the offer!'

With that he had stooped to gather her up and fling her across the bed. She was still in her slip and bra and he pinioned her protesting hands while he wrenched them off her.

'Grant, don't! You're angry with me; you can't want to——!'

'Make love? As long as *you* don't want to, that's O.K. with me,' he had muttered thickly. 'Since you hate being married to me, you may as well have something to remember to hate me for.'

'If you force me, you're going to hate yourself!'

'I'll risk that.'

In vain she had turned her head this way and

that to avoid the brutish bruising kisses which assaulted her mouth. Grant caught at her chin to steady it while his weight crowded her, making her body his prisoner. He had not attempted to rouse her either by gentle exploratory touch or with the murmured love-words they had invented for themselves. She protested no further and he did not speak. When she knew he was about to take his will of her she would not embrace him, and she dared her body either to welcome him or enjoy him. Tonight she would not meet this punishing, calculated act of desire with her own sweet surge of ecstasy as answer. Grant had cheapened her, first with words and now with this cruel rape had debased her further. If he had really meant that as his parting gesture to her then he should remember it for the ugly, arid thing it was with as much shame as he had forced on her. But he couldn't have meant that— could he?

To her surprise and utter chagrin she had had to learn that he had. They had not argued the issue of her accompanying him again, and with the shortest of preliminaries and preparation he had left alone for the Persian Gulf as part troubleshooter for the Opal Oil plants still working out their concessions from the Arab authorities, part adviser to the same authorities, and part pupil to the experts on offshore installations. He had taken his shift leaves on site and his two-yearly furloughs, one on safari in Africa, and one in Japan. They had not met again, and after long weary days and lonely nights of suffering and hiding the ache she felt for him, Fern had gradually grown a kind of crust over her feelings. From being at first a hermit crab, retreated into the protection of a shell, she had emerged as the vivacious leader of her social set, ready to try anything once and, failing or succeeding, going on to the next stimulant without looking back.

And now, tonight, two or three hours hence, she had been tricked into meeting Grant again. Under her father's critical eye, under Grant's appraising stare. She was glad he had been tricked into it too. Sir Manfred had urged her to look her 'prettiest'—his generation's word for 'glamorous' in her own. Well, she *would*. Grant should have an eyeful. In the thirty months of their separation she had grown up, been made aware of her feminine power, learned that such looks and poise as she had could be used to advantage—— Her thoughts veered. How would Grant have changed in the same time? Did she want to find him changed? She didn't know.

She went to her cabin and took a long time to change after deciding to wear a trouser suit of thick white silk which enhanced her suntan. Bra and crêpe-de-chine briefs beneath the suit and bare feet in sandals which were no more than an intricacy of narrow thongs. Freshly tubbed and glowing, she sat at her dressing-shelf in the nude, studying what Grant would see of her when they met.

She ran her fingers into her hair, lifting it and spreading it and allowing it to fall naturally about her face. Newly-born, she had been christened Fern before anyone could have known her baby-blue eyes would turn to their rare, lustrous green.

Inspired guess on the part of her parents! She had been more complimented on the apt link between her name and her heavily fringed green eyes than on any other feature. Of these there were a delicate nose, high-boned cheeks, a mobile mouth and a proud column of throat and neck. Her skin was flawlessly transparent beneath her tan—'mother-of-pearl see-through', Grant had once described it—and she needed little make-up except a soft green eyeshadow and some lip colour for evening, which she used now.

For the rest, she was long-legged and slim-hipped—she stood and ran her hands from breast to thigh before completing her minimum of dressing. She would have been hypocritical if she hadn't known she had more than her share of young beauty and wealth. But where had either got her? Into an ecstatically rapturous marriage, brief as a honeymoon before it had soured, and since into an enforced grass-widowhood inevitably tarnished by temptation to sexual adventures which so far she had managed to resist. Hadn't Grant realised what he was abandoning her to when he had left her? And how much temptation hadn't he even tried to resist, being a man and entitled by male tradition to footloose experiment?

As always, she forced her mind to close against that picture—of another woman, other women, in Grant's arms, but she was taut with nerves when Sir Manfred came to her cabin to take her to the main saloon where his steward was waiting to serve drinks from the bar.

By now *Calypso* had been edged in to her berth

at the dock, and while her father took a drink and chatted with the steward Fern went to look out of a window which gave a view of the quay. The tropic sun had set, the daytime bustle of work had stopped. Down there only a group of three or four Lascars squatted on their haunches gossiping, until a long open car came down the quay, when they sprang up to open doors in the hope of a tip.

Fern took one glance at the car and turned back to the saloon.

'Grant,' she breathed. 'Driving, and—people with him.'

Sir Manfred's reaction was explicit. 'Hell,' he said. 'I should have warned Grant I expected him alone. Who? How many?'

'Another man and a woman.'

'Let me see——' Sir Manfred turned to announce, 'Austin Logan and his wife. They're coming aboard with Grant. This is tricky.'

Fern said grimly, 'Too tricky by half. If you think I'm to be brought face to face with Grant in front of witnesses, you're mistaken.'

'He'll have to know you're here!'

'Too bad, then, isn't it, that once he knows, he'll have to wait to see me? I'm going back to my cabin to change, and I shall go ashore.'

'You'll do nothing of the kind, my girl—ashore, alone at night on an island where you've never set foot?'

'Then I'll go to bed and lock my cabin door.'

'You haven't time. You could meet them on the companionway. Leave me to handle it——'

She had to. Sir Manfred had broken off just as

the door was opened by a steward showing in Grant and the two people Fern did not know. He stepped forward, hands outstretched, slightly obscuring her. 'Logan—and Mrs Logan—we haven't met, have we? Welcome to *Calypso*, the Company yacht. And Wilder—Grant, my boy, look who's come with me for a holiday on Maracca while I have to be here——'

The studiedly bright tone died away, and for a moment the five of them stood, silent, as if in tableau. Then Grant stepped forward, his hand offered to Fern. His smile for her was polite, coolly welcoming. He said. 'Fern Stirling—surprise, surprise!' then, dropping her hand, turned to his companions. 'Miss Stirling, Sir Manfred's daughter, Mrs Logan,' he introduced her, his glance at his chief a challenge which Sir Manfred did not take up, though his frown and his sharp-drawn breath betrayed shock.

In that previous moment of silence, Fern's and Grant's eyes had met, searching and searched. For Fern, time had rolled back to the instant of her first sight of this craggy, bronzed man; to that wordless awareness which had told her that, if fortune were good to her, here was her fate. Now the strong, expressively lined face under the thatch of dark brown hair had not changed, nor had the body whose contours and virile hardnesses she had come to know so well in the few months of their closeness in marriage. He was Grant, her husband, still there for her within touch and hearing——

But green eyes had to fall before the steely-cold provocation of grey. By that cold acknowledgement and introduction of her by her maiden name he had disowned her as his wife! What did he mean by it? How *dared* he humiliate her so? She looked at her father. Surely he wouldn't let Grant get away with such an insult to her? Or—the ugly suspicion struck—had he perhaps known Grant was going to deny her right to his name? No, for Sir Manfred hadn't expected anyone else to be present when she and Grant met, so that his look of bewilderment at Grant's announcement must be genuine. And when he looked at her directly with an almost imperceptible shake of his head, she guessed he meant to make no comment in front of the Logans, and was asking her to make none either.

Though she was raging within, for pride's sake she obeyed. In fact she brought all her dramatic sense to playing the part which Grant's revenge had allotted to her. Smiling, she gave her hand to Mrs Logan. 'Maracca looks a beautiful island— you'll have to show me the sights,' she said, and then sweetly to Grant, 'Yes, I daresay you were surprised that I dragged myself away from London. But let's see—it must be quite a time since we met? You were last in England—m'm— two years ago? Less? More?' A little shrug. 'One sees so many people coming and going at Opal that one loses count!'

'More than two years—nearer three, except for the odd call to make a report or for a briefing.' Grant's face was a mask.

'Oh, yes,' Fern agreed carelessly. 'I think I heard you looked in occasionally for the one-night stand, with no time to spare for socialising. Such devotion to duty!' She turned again to the Logans. 'After Grant went to—where was it, the Gulf?' she appealed to Grant—'you'd never believe how he dropped out of things. He left us all agog, wondering whether it was mounting ambition that was biting him, or whether he'd been turned down by some girl and he'd welcomed the chance to get away to "forget"!'

She saw the dark storm on Grant's face and felt headily rewarded. Her knife-thrust of malice had gone home! But he did not retaliate. He ignored her to tell Sir Manfred his choice of drinks. The Logans chose theirs, and with creditable ease of manner Sir Manfred guided the talk into an exchange of Company news, an account of *Calypso*'s voyage, and the discussion of plans for their stay—mostly business ones for him, social ones for Fern.

Mrs Logan, a tall spare woman with a weathered skin, sharp features and rather cold eyes, promised Fern some introductions to the island's European community, though warning her, 'You'll find we're not much more than the thin filling in a thick sandwich of Malays and Indians and island-born Maraccans,' which brought a nod of agreement from her husband, but from Grant the dry comment, 'After all, the sandwich was here before we were,' and from Sir Manfred a confident, 'Sandwich and filling, we both need each other, and it's not going to be the fault of Opal's youngest enterprise if, with Grant in charge, we don't slot in together very well.'

At which Mrs Logan glanced first at Grant and then at her husband. 'We have to hope so,' she

said on an edge of seeming doubt which told
Fern's sixth sense that in his colleague's wife,
Grant had an enemy. Why? And in finding herself
on the defensive for Grant against this sour
woman there was an even more contradictory
Why?

Austin Logan was asking Sir Manfred, 'Will
you be camping on board, sir?', getting the reply,
'Oh yes, I think so. Fern and I are settled in our
cabins; there's room to entertain here in the
saloon, and——' Sir Manfred grinned, 'since I've
commandeered the yacht for six weeks or so, our
shareholders will expect me to make full hotel use
of her! Before you go, I'll show you over her.
She's quite a gal.'

Soon after that, at the Logans' murmur about
leaving, Fern made it an opportunity to refuse
another drink, saying she was tired after the last
twenty-four hours' run from Mauritius, and
would they excuse her if she went to her cabin
and to early bed?

'Dinner?' asked her father.

'I'm not very hungry, but I'll have a tray in my
cabin if I want anything.'

'Very well.' He didn't press her, for which she
was grateful. He must know it was her way of
escaping from Grant, he had to be on her side.
She shared a smile between the others. The
Logans said no more about going and Grant
crossed the floor in a couple or three strides to
open the door for her.

'Goodnight, Miss Stirling,' he said. She did not
reply and swept past him.

In her cabin she sank down on her bed, hands

clenched between her knees, and let her thoughts run angry riot, veering against Sir Manfred and Grant in turn.

That phoney scheme of her father's, in trying to spring her on Grant like a rabbit from a conjuror's hat! Well, he had been hoist with it, and she *almost* wasn't sorry it had turned on him and bitten him. But it had also bitten her. Grant had outplayed them both, and at the very instant of his setting eyes upon her again.

An instantaneous reaction of contempt for her. No hesitation at all, simply that bland, 'Fern Stirling—surprise, surprise!'—putting her publicly where he considered she belonged, out of his life, out of any claim to his recent thoughts or any implied need of her.

She had done her best to pay him out, and thought she had momentarily succeeded. But not for long. He had rebounded with his further taunt at the door of the saloon, and where and how far did he mean to carry this denial of her as his wife? He had sounded so sure of himself, and the Logans hadn't questioned it, which could mean he was masquerading as a bachelor in Maracca, and where did that leave *her*?

He had brought the Logans with him, so presumably they would be leaving together, and her father would come to her, she felt sure. She stepped out of her suit, discarded bra and briefs and padded to her bathroom, taking her wisp of a nightgown with her. Her cabin steward had turned down her bed and adjusted the mosquito net. She got into bed, drawing the necessary single sheet over her and deciding against bothering with dinner. While she waited for Sir Manfred she was too strung up to read, but sleep must have overtaken her, for when she woke with a start the hands of her luminous bedside clock had moved on to ten o'clock and there was a tapping at her door.

She responded drowsily, 'Is that you, Father? Just a minute——' and threw back the sheet. But her feet hadn't swung to the floor when a voice said, 'It's not the Chief. Grant.' A pause. 'Remember me?'

Fully awake now, she tensed, her heart thudding. 'Go away,' she called. 'I've gone to bed and I don't want to be disturbed.'

A small silence, then—'So warns this card on your door-handle. But circumstances are exceptional, wouldn't you agree?'

Fern pondered this, then said pertly, 'I didn't choose the circumstances. You did.'

'Wrong. They were thrust upon me by your father, as you very well know.'

'Then go and talk to him about them, and leave me alone.'

'He and I have already discussed them, and now I'm reporting to you. So do I get your boy to use his pass-key, or do I force the lock, or do you turn the key yourself? Take your choice.'

She had none, and he knew it. She slipped out of bed, went to the door and turned the key. Grant did the rest, and they faced each other on the threshold, he at the advantage of having got his way, she with the handicap of being barefoot, too flimsily attired for dignity and having been bested by his will.

He came into the cabin, closing the door behind him. 'You'd better get back into bed or put on some more clothes,' he said. 'This is merely a committee of ways and means. Seduction isn't on my programme tonight.'

CHAPTER TWO

'ANY more than letting you seduce me is on mine.'
Turning, Fern slid her feet into mules and went
to a cupboard for a robe. Tying its sash, she
glanced at Grant from beneath her lashes. Did he
feel none of the tingling undercurrent of excitement and apprehension that was running through
her own veins? she wondered as she sat down on
the bed. He took the only chair.

'How could you have talked to Father in front
of those people?' she asked.

'I didn't. I drove them home, and came back to
dine at his invitation.'

'I wonder you had the gall to accept!'

'He'd made it more of an order than an invitation, and after all, I'd been drinking his whisky,
so sharing a crust with him didn't seem much
more of a crime.'

'He could at least have come to tell *me* he was
having you to dinner!'

'Yes, well—a just man, your father. Believes in
giving the guilty party a hearing—a grace which
he probably knew this party wouldn't get from
you.' Grant paused. 'Of course he was spoiling
for a fight on your behalf, but between the soup
and the coffee he gradually came round, and over
his last cigar he conceded that I was justified.'

'*Justified?* In repudiating me as you did?' Fern
protested.

'Justified in reverting to my single status when you left me,' Grant corrected.

'When *you* left *me*.' Fern worked it out. 'You mean—you've let people think you're not married, ever since you went away without me that time?'

A nod. 'Ever since. It's saved my having to excuse your not being with me, and the freedom of bachelordom affords a nice line in fringe benefits, I've found.'

'I daresay. As many affairs as you regretted having bypassed when you married me! You could have had "any woman, and no pack-drill", you said, and playing bachelor must have given you a lot of scope,' Fern taunted.

Grant said, 'You have too long a memory for your own comfort, my dear. But though I'd be flattered to think I could make you jealous, I doubt if you've lost very much sleep in torment over the few recreations which, being offered, were sometimes accepted.'

'And you'd be right at that,' she lied.

'I thought as much. Three years is a long time, and according to her father the little self-appointed grass widow didn't mourn her loss for long. Into every brand of silliness there was— river parties at Maidenhead, to which the police were called more than once, a stab at hiring a stall in the Antiques Market, which lost treble the value of the things it sold, a punch-up over you at one of the currently "in" night-clubs. According to the Chief the list is legion, and in their mongering of "When the cat's away" stories the gossip-column writers have had themselves a ball;

every story a snide hit at "the Opal heiress whose husband is seldom seen around town—etc., etc." No, I don't think our split exactly broke your heart,' Grant finished cuttingly.

'Well, at least I didn't deny I had a husband; I didn't ignore your existence as you did mine,' Fern countered furiously. '*I* had to take the snide bits on the chin, while you'd swanned off to the Persian Gulf or wherever, pretending to all your floozies that you were a single man. And what did you expect me to do? I'd gone home where I wasn't needed. You hadn't even left me my own place to look after. I didn't waste all my time—I gave a bunch of children some French lessons— and what was wrong in my filling up the rest of it by looking for some fun with my set?'

Knowing she was putting questions which he would sidestep if he could, she paused for breath, then attacked again with, 'Anyway, what right had you to discuss me with Father? How did he come to complain about me to you?'

Grant did answer that one. 'You don't seem to realise that you had worried him stiff until he hit on the idea of dangling the carrot of Maracca before you, guessing you might grab at it, which you did. His optimism had told him, "Throw the two of them together again, and they'll jell"—not reckoning, of course, with the fact that for three years I've claimed no ownership of a wife from whom I've had neither comfort nor service, and that his bringing you here on a holiday hasn't altered the position at all.'

'You mean——' Fern hesitated '——that, even if the Logans hadn't been there, you would still have—have disowned me?'

'Not quite so formally, of course. But yes,' Grant agreed, 'I'd have left you and your father in no doubt that a reunion isn't on while the situation holds—of your being merely on a joy-flip to Maracca, and of my being prepared to sit it out as a bachelor until—if ever—you're willing to meet my terms.'

'As if I'd dream of it under threat!' she defied.

'As if——' he echoed. 'As if, in fact, you find yourself with the slightest intention of rejoining me, threat or no threat. Which makes us of one mind, though I'm afraid you're going to have to get used to being publicly "disowned" as my wife while you're here.'

'You're carrying on the fiction you made up for the Logans—that I'm——?'

'Still the lovely Fern Stirling, fair game for amorous bachelors, I'm afraid,' Grant finished for her, as he stood. 'That's what the committee of ways and means has had to be about. That's what I came to tell you,' he said, making for the door.

In a strangely perverse way disappointment stirred her as she watched him go.

Fern had waited until after midnight for her father to come to see her after Grant had left. But the yacht had settled down to silence, and at last she had to acknowledge that Grant must have persuaded him he could do nothing to add to nor subtract from Grant's ultimatum to her, and he had—only temporarily, surely?—taken the coward's way out.

Well, there was something *she* could do about

it, she was thinking stormily as she dressed the next morning. Each day on the voyage out she had gone to breakfast with her father in his cabin. He couldn't escape her there, and was she going to leave him in any doubt at all as to the consequences of yesterday's coup? *Was* she!

Her first setback was to find he had already breakfasted without her, had set aside his tray and was working on some papers on a desk-flap; her second, that he did not immediately look up at her entrance, but only murmured an absent, 'Just a minute, love,' when she was ready to explode.

'*Father!* Well, honestly, anyone would think you weren't even there when Grant insulted me last night!' she protested hotly. 'But you heard him. You let him get away with it, and then—*then* you went into league with him over dinner, and as far as I can gather, as good as patted him on the head and told him he'd been right to do it!'

At that Sir Manfred did draw down heavy hornrims to look at her over them. Removing and polishing them, he said, 'You're wrong there. I couldn't approve it, and I was as taken aback as you were. But I did appreciate later, when he explained himself that with the Logans there, there was nothing else he could do.'

'The Logans! He's admitted to me that if we'd been alone, he'd have told us he's posed as single ever since he left me, and means to go on doing it, unless——'

'Unless?'

'Unless I go back to him unconditionally, of course.'

'And are you going back to him?'

Pertly—'With a pistol at my head, what do you think?' Fern retorted. 'I'd rather die.'

'Don't be extravagant,' her father rebuked. 'Does he want you back?'

'You seem to be in each other's confidence, why don't you ask him?'

'I shouldn't dream of it. If you still had any sensitivity about him, you'd know yourself. Meanwhile, as I told you, I've brought you, however clumsily, within arm's length of each other, and now I'm washing my hands—Reminding you, though, that as long as he does no harm by it, a man may describe himself as he pleases.'

'And his wife as the spinster which she isn't, I suppose?'

'I'm afraid it follows, if they have to meet each other, or mix with people they both know.' Sir Manfred swivelled his chair and sat knee to knee with her, laying a hand on her lap. 'But in your case, love, there's a remedy available if you care to take it. That is, if you're convinced there's no hope for my poor scheme, I can lay it on for you in a couple of hours. You have only to say.'

Fern looked down at his hand, took it and pressed it. He meant so well, and he loved her, she knew. Less truculently but doubtfully, she asked, 'What remedy? What do you mean?'

'That you needn't see Grant again. I'll have Captain Lewis do a turnaround with *Calypso* and take you back to Durban, where you can book a flight home. How about that?'

She had listened wonderingly. 'Go back to

England when we've only just arrived?' she questioned.

'Only you. I must stay to do what I came for, and Lewis will come back for me. I can go to a hotel while *Calypso* is away.'

'But what about my holiday here? I was looking forward to it. No,' Fern decided for herself, 'I'm not afraid of Grant, and I'm not running away from him. He'll just have to get used to seeing me around—at the distance I shall keep him.'

Sir Manfred patted her hand. 'Bravely said! I'm glad you don't want to go. But avoiding Grant isn't going to be so easy. Apart from my having to see a lot of him, we shall be meeting him socially; wherever we're invited, as the future chief of Opal here, he'll be invited too, and whenever I do any entertaining myself, he'll have to be there. So have any second thoughts you like, my love. I shall understand.'

'I don't want any,' Fern maintained woodenly. 'I came here for a holiday, and I'm going to have it. And if Grant wants to get too close—in any way—I daresay I can always freeze him out.'

'As, without noticeable effect, you tried to do last night,' her father reminded her. 'You sounded so waspish, I was ashamed of you.'

'Yes, well—he'd asked for it. I wasn't going to have him think I'd spent the best part of three years missing him!'

'If he ever did think or hope so, I was able to disabuse him of that idea.'

Fern nodded. 'Yes, I know. You told him all about some of the fun scrapes I got into. As if any of them were serious! And anyway, Father, whose side are you on?'

Sir Manfred sighed and turned back to his papers. 'Old fool that I am, I'd supposed that by now I shouldn't have to take sides; that between you and Grant there wouldn't *be* two sides, just one.'

'But now you know there are two—whose?' she persisted.

His look at her was one of gentle rebuke, shaming her. 'You shouldn't have to ask,' he told her, adding more briskly, 'Run along now and get dressed—something very cool but which will cover you, and a hat. The Maraccan sun can be cruel, and out on the Opal site where Grant is taking us this morning, there'll be little or no shade.'

Dismissed, Fern paused at the door to put a question. 'How is it the Logans didn't know Grant is married to me?'

'Ah, that——' her father replied. 'They came into Opal directly from Canada, long after your marriage was news, and only Austin has been to London for briefing once.'

'I see. And——?' But there, about to ask something else, Fern checked. 'Nothing,' she told her father's raised eyebrows, and went out. She had been about to say, 'I suppose, if Grant is having an affair with someone on the island, he must have a *very* vested interest in repudiating me?' But she had decided in time to keep this suspicion to herself. She was on her own in this. For if he were keeping a mistress or even merely dallying, she could prove more of a thorn in his flesh by keeping close enough to him to annoy him and her rival than by avoiding him as she had planned.

She felt a certain wicked glee at the thought, and last night's tingle of expectant excitement came back.

The dock area of Port Dauphin, the island's capital town, was no more attractive than any dockland; a place of corrugated iron sheds and warehouses, burning pavements and an airless atmosphere pervaded by the mingled odours of stored copra, sugar, coffee and rubber awaiting shipment abroad.

But Grant's big open car, broad enough for him and his two passengers abreast, soon gained the broad tree-lined and flower-bedecked boulevards of the town, crowded with tourist strollers, cars, dark-skinned women carrying bundles and pitchers upon their heads, men trundling primitive carts and children underfoot everywhere. The sky was an inverted blue bowl with a few light clouds for ornament; the villas of the residential quarters a dazzle of white against the palettes of brilliant colour which were their gardens.

Farther afield still the country was green and empty, opening out gradually towards the extreme tip of the island which was the land site of the oil camp, with embryo drilling platforms a short way out to sea and a smaller dock than Port Dauphin, for tankers to be refilled or to discharge crude oil for refining.

By contrast with the luscious scenery of the rest of Maracca the area was one of harsh commercialism—fleets of derricks, tall cracking towers, maintenance sheds and offices, and Fern, who had been ecstatic over the alien, exotic scene, felt a peevish desire to criticise this, Grant's own domain.

Speaking *to* her father but *at* Grant, she commented, 'What a pity you had to spoil a lovely island like Maracca—cutting up the land, disturbing the people, polluting the air—I wonder you have the nerve!'

Sir Manfred looked across her head at Grant, and it was Grant who replied.

'And how long do you suppose tiny dots like Maracca are going to survive into the next century on their self-supporting crops of coconut oil and cane sugar and real rubber and coffee, of which, as often as not, there's a world surplus for burning?' he demanded.

'They seem to have done well enough up to now.'

'But may not much longer without our help— to find and work the stuff that the world is needing and will go to war for to get. Maracca is lucky——'

'And at most we're encroaching on less than a square mile of it,' put in Sir Manfred. 'Giving work to hundreds, schooling their children, paying them well. You must show Fern round the joint while I'm getting down to cases with Logan in the office,' he told Grant.

They parted company when Grant drew up outside a one-storey white building facing a heat-browned lawn bordered by scarlet ixoras. Sir Manfred alighted and went in. Grant drove slowly on, describing the camp's layout on the way. The marshalling yards, crossed and recrossed by trunk railway lines, repair sheds, welding shops, the main on-shore drilling rigs, the several-platformed columns, flanked by thin chimneys, from which at night the continuous flare resembled the fire under a devil's cauldron,' Grant remarked.

This was the centre of the camp. Good smooth roads radiated out from it; branch road foundations were still being dug. A quarter of a mile from the offices there were tennis courts, a swimming-pool, and about there the neat avenues of staff bungalows began.

'Quarters for the married Europeans, mostly,' Grant pointed them out. 'There's a bachelors' club, Le Corsair, nearer in to camp.'

'Where do you live?' Fern asked.

'At the Club when I have to sleep on site, but I keep a studio-apartment in town which I use on occasion.'

'Occasions—such as?' she probed.

'Use your imagination. Late night parties, car going on the blink——'

'And dates?'

'I told you to use your imagination. Such occasions have been known,' he said coolly.

'By "town", do you mean Port Dauphin? Where is it, your flat?'

'It's a kind of tiny penthouse over the Hotel Meurice, where I think Sir Manfred plans to take you to lunch today. Why? Thinking of visiting me there uninvited?'

Ignoring the gibe, 'Just that Father and I ought to know where to find you,' she said, and changed the subject. Watching the tinies playing in the handkerchief-sized gardens and the young mothers in the scantiest of shorts and halter-tops going in and out of their houses, she remarked of the camp, 'It's all like a very new town, not finished, but self-contained, and these are the suburbs.'

Grant nodded. 'It was planned that way. There's a library—mostly paperbacks people have given—and a clinic and a crèche, and of course the Club bar——'

'And a school?'

'Only nursery. The older children mostly go back to boarding schools in Europe. We're even favoured by a prevailing wind which carries the polluting fumes you were so scornful about out to sea.' He had halted the car and now he half-turned towards her, his arm over the back of his seat. 'Not quite as sordid a pad as you expected? Rather a pity you judged my job by the rigours of Canada and the Gulf. You might have been bribed by Maracca to stay with me, if we'd found oil here earlier than we did. There's hardly a travel brochure on the market that can resist calling it "this island paradise".'

She would not let him think she was bedazzled by Maracca. 'I'd still rather Opal had based you in London, where everything is going. I told you at the time Father would have fixed it, if you'd let me ask him. He would even now——'

The corner of Grant's mouth lifted in a half-smile. 'Tenacious little string-puller, aren't you? You never give up,' he mocked her. 'That's the price you set on yourself—that I heave myself behind a desk at Head Office, and you will allow—what do they call them?—conjugal relations to be resumed?' He shook his head and turned front again. 'Oh no, my girl, we aren't trading that way—we've already been through it all. And though you're as seductive as you ever were, you're still about as immature as a green hazelnut. You knew what my job was soon after I first kissed you, but you saw marriage as a great big sugar-coated bonbon, and me as a guy whose spots you could change as soon as you walked him out of the church lych-gate. And you're still thinking the same—you've only to wheedle the Chief and——'

'I'm not, I'm not,' she denied hotly. 'I only said Father would reconsider, but if you think I'm going to beg him, you're mistaken. I wouldn't and I won't lift a finger to persuade you to alter a single plan you've made for yourself and your future. As for me'—self-pity quivered her lip, but she controlled it—'Father tricked me into coming, but now I'm here, I'm going to have my holiday and enjoy it without any obligations to you, Grant Wilder—*bachelor*!'

'Good. All power to your pretty elbow, although——'

'Stop *flattering* me!'

'Impossible. You know precisely the heady effect you create; you've been working on it since you were in your cradle.' He restarted the car, and continued, 'I was about to say you may have to find yourself more beholden to me than is likely to please you.'

'How so?'

'Socially, I mean. You'll need introductions to the local personnel, and who, it will be thought, more fitting to escort the Chief's daughter initially than Opal's principal man in Maracca? Yes, I'm afraid you'll have to get used to seeing me around.'

'On the social beat? I thought you worked for a living?' she scoffed.

'To sink, worn out, on my bachelor's wooden pallet at the early evening hour at which the tropics go to bed? No, I do manage to keep a reserve of energy on tap for the odd dance or dining out at night.'

'Or the odd date?'

'And/or date. Dinner first, dalliance afterwards.'

'In the penthouse upstairs at the Meurice?'

'Sometimes. Alternatively, we have plenty of deserted beaches and as periodic moonlight as anywhere else.'

'Of course—all the romantic amenities! Well, even if you have to make a duty of sponsoring me, don't let me interrupt anything, will you?' she snapped.

In the swift glance he threw at her there was a demonic glint she recognised. 'What possible reason could you have for wanting to?' he questioned unanswerably.

Fern could have told him if she would. There was a word for it. For all the bitterness between them, keeping them apart, she could still be as jealous of him as if she still possessed him.

From beneath the cartwheel brim of her straw hat she watched him covertly as he drove—hands expertly at their job, bronzed profile turned to her, athletic torso from which her imagination

stripped the thin shirting which hid it ...
His hands, caressing another woman's hair,
shoulders, breasts. *His* head, bent in study of
a face he meant to kiss. *His* body, relaxed
upon heat-soaked or moon-shafted sands; a body,
not hers, beside it. Grant, dancing with someone
else, limbs in taut, lean movement which the other
had to follow, obedient to their leadership, sub-
jugated to his will while the dance lasted and the
rhythm beat—No! Only this morning she had
thought she could watch that happening, but now
she doubted if she could bear it. She had to
hope he would be discreet, but she doubted if he
would be. That look she had caught had been
meant as a dare to her to show she had feelings
which he could still hurt, because to do so would
lend spice to an affair. He claimed to believe
she didn't care, but he would like to goad her
into a waspishness which betrayed that she was
jealous. She was going to have to guard against
that.

Sir Manfred was waiting for them outside the
office block. 'You will lunch with us?' he asked
Grant, who agreed that he would like to.

The Meurice had an elegance all its own. It
was a long white colonnaded building with a
frontage to a wide boulevard and a depth running
back to a stone-balconied façade overlooking the
sea. The immense dining-room ran this whole
length, with lunch tables for choice out on the
balcony, where a table was reserved for Sir
Manfred.

'Grant must advise us on a Maraccan meal,' he
told Fern. 'As I remember, it will be a mixture of

Chinese and Indian and local. Isn't that so?' he
referred to Grant.

It was as strangely assorted food as Fern had
ever had put before her. She supposed the thin,
tepid, faintly scented soup was the first course,
but it stayed to be sipped as a thirst-quencher
throughout the meal. About each place there was
a crescent of tiny side-dishes of sliced eggs, nuts,
prawns and bean shoots in delicate sauces, to be
taken alongside an ochre-coloured curry poured
over a bowl of rice. The only familiar offering of
any was a fruit salad of mangoes and lichees and
melon slices.

The men watched her experimental tasting and
savouring with interest. 'Don't worry that you'll
always feed like this,' Grant advised drily. 'At a
lower level of cuisine it could all come out of tins
or be chicken ad nauseam. And you'd better like
avocadoes—or else! You'll have them stuffed with
everything.'

He and Sir Manfred talked business as they ate.
'How was Logan?' Grant asked.

'None too pleased about your taking over.
You'll need to be diplomatic. He feels his nose
has been put out of joint.'

'That's Freda Logan talking. Beside her, Austin
is a negative quantity. But she's as ambitious for
him as a mother hen,' said Grant, confirming
Fern's hunch that he had no friend in Mrs Logan.

'Aha! "The female of the species——" ' Sir
Manfred was beginning to quote, but stopped
when both he and Fern saw that he had lost
Grant's attention.

Fern followed Grant's glance. It was directed

at the slim grace of the woman approaching their
table, a smile dawning on her lips and a hand
theatrically offered at arm's length to Grant as he
rose from his chair. She was a redhead, the rich
fall of her hair drawn to lie cloakwise on one bare
shoulder; on the other a huge green bow supported the slanting line of a green sundress. Her skin
was deeply olive, her eyes hidden behind wing-
framed sunglasses. When Grant gave her his hand
she held on to it, lightly pumping it up and down
as she scolded in English just touched with a
French accent, 'They say there are none so blind
as those who won't see, and *who* didn't spare a
glance for the poor de Mille, gnawing a lonely
crust in the dining-room as he came through—
with his friends?'

Grant laughed, put his lips to her hand and
released it. 'How could I have missed you?' he
parried. 'You must blame my friends; they
obscured my vision.'

'Of course. Understandable.' Momentarily
the sunglasses were turned on Fern, then on
Sir Manfred. 'But introduce me now, won't
you?'

Grant murmured names. 'Sir Manfred Stirling,
my chief, Miss Fern Stirling, his daughter—
Mademoiselle Rose de Mille, who's doing a
season here at the Meurice between her last in
Berlin and her next in Athens——'

De Mille. Now Fern understood why the new-
comer had described herself so. For in the foyer
there had been a large easel, advertising—La de
Mille. World-Famous Folk Singer in Six
Languages. Recitals Each Evening in the

Golden Mosque Room at 21 hrs, and on Gala Nights at Midnight.

So! Famous enough in her own field to be known by her surname like Garbo or Fonteyn, a beauty, here at the Meurice, and obviously on familiar terms with Grant. Fern was wondering if she need look farther for a rival when she noticed that the outsize sunglasses were off and she was being studied by liquid brown eyes as their owner told Sir Manfred,

'Grant had told me he was expecting you, but he hadn't said you were bringing your daughter.'

'No. He didn't know she would be coming with me—a holiday for her which I hope she'll enjoy.'

'Oh, I am sure! Maracca is a lovely island, so exotic, so romantic,' enthused Rose de Mille. She turned back to Grant. 'You hadn't mentioned Miss Stirling to me, but you would have known each other in England?'

A corner of Grant's mouth twitched. 'Yes, very well,' he said.

'Aah——!' The long-drawn monosyllable and the knowing smile which accompanied it were arch to a degree. And her pretence of welcome about as false as a Judas kiss, thought Fern acidly, debating the effect she could create if to Grant's dry admission she added her own, 'Well, naturally—since we are married.' But half longing, half fearing to do it, she refrained. The time was not ripe for it yet.

Seemingly content with whatever she had gained from the encounter, Rose de Mille was taking her leave, refusing Sir Manfred's suggestion that she should join them for coffee. Her brilliant smile embraced the three of them as she asked, 'You will all be at the Gala tonight? Grant, you will be escorting Miss Stirling?'

'If Fern would like to come.'

'But of course she would—with *you*,' Rose claimed, her emphasis implying that Fern should consider herself lucky to have as enviable a partner as Grant laid on for her without even trying.

When she had gone Grant furnished a thumbnail sketch of her background. Half French, half American, with a touch of Dutch Indonesian blood, she had studied in America and Germany, and had a wide repertoire of folk and intimate songs. She travelled with her accompanist, a woman guitarist named Sophie Dean who acted also as her dresser and secretary.

In answer to Sir Manfred's question, 'Yes, she has a suite here in the hotel for the season,' Grant told him, and answering Fern's reluctant praise of her glamour, said, 'Yes, quite a looker, and as talented as they come. Unmarried? One is given to suppose so, but one doesn't ask.'

After lunch Grant drove back to *Calypso* and he and Sir Manfred had returned to the site, while Fern had turned in for a long siesta. Now she was dressing for the gala evening, having failed to convince her father that she need not go.

'Of course you'll go,' he had told her over their evening drink in the saloon. 'I shan't. I've brought back work to do, and I shall have an early night. But to dance and have fun is what you came for, and as Grant is the only man you know so far, I want you to go with him.'

'In disguise—as "Miss Fern Stirling"?'

'Since that's the way you both seem to want it, yes. Although——' Sir Manfred had paused, 'I did give you marks for your control of your tongue this afternoon. I got the impression you had to bite on it to stop yourself from contradicting Grant when he introduced you, which would have embarrassed us all.' He had looked anxiously into her face. 'Do you think you're going to be able to take other hurdles of the same sort? Or would you like to change your mind and fly home?'

Fern had clenched her teeth. 'I'm staying as long as you do,' she said. 'Grant isn't driving me out.'

Now, getting ready for Grant to call for her, she debated whether to try to outdo Rose de Mille in glamour—which she probably could, from the collection of haute couture clothes she had brought with her—or to create an effect by the contrast of the most simple dress she had, a high-waisted style in white chiffon, with tiny ruched sleeves and a demure pie-dish frill at the neck. She drew back her hair severely off her face and bunched it in Jane Austen ringlets behind the crown of her head. She wore a single string of pearls, a wedding gift from her father, and looking down at the hand from which she had angrily wrenched her ring last night, wished she had thought of making that defiant gesture in front of Grant. Failing that, there ought to be some way in which she could bring home to him that, though she outwardly accepted his sponsorship and his company when she had to, her rejection of him was as uncompromising as his was of her.

Before she went to meet him in the saloon, she had thought of something. The ring went with her in her evening bag.

A gala night at the Meurice was obviously an important social occasion for Port Dauphin. A long line of cars queued at the entrance which was carnival-lit and carpeted down to the edge of the pavement. There was a gaily noisy crush of people in the foyer, and after failing to crowd their way into one of the several bars, Grant put a firm hand beneath Fern's elbow, urging her to the elevators.

'We'll make it like a couple of solitary drinkers upstairs,' he said. 'Leave them to sort themselves out.'

They shot swiftly up four floors—'No skyscrapers on Maracca. The typhoon risk, though remote, is too great'—Grant remarked as they emerged on to a corridor at the lift-shaft's limit.

He unlocked a door and showed Fern into a living room furnished, like many Eastern rooms, with a minimum of pieces—high-backed carved chairs in black oak, a bureau, a carved coffee table and rush mats for the marble floor. Its windows looked out over the sea, and through half open doors Fern glimpsed a kitchen and a bedroom.

Grant went to a cabinet, poured rum and lime juice, added ice from a canteen and brought it to her.

'This is your pad?' she asked.

He nodded. 'Strictly utility-equipped by the management, as you see. No tiger skins or silken divans for the wooing of houris. But there's a double bed.'

'Indeed?'

'Not interested? Of course, I should have known. Then in the interests of seduction, I can only offer you the view, I'm afraid.'

Fern went over to the window to look down through the branches of palm trees at the expanse of sea, coloured under the darkening evening sky in blues and purples and still the red-gold traces of reflection of a sunset already over. She stood watching it in silence until the colours faded and the swift darkness of the East came down, blotting them out.

At her elbow Grant queried, 'No comment?'

'It's lovely—out of this world,' she murmured.

'Doesn't it occur to you that if you'd been less lily-livered and more tolerant of my job, you could have earned this in time as legitimately as I did?'

Her moment of softening passed. 'I daresay— at the price of enduring Canada and the Gulf and—and no doubt the north of Scotland in winter or wherever, before I achieved it? Why *should* I have had to "earn" it with miseries like that?' she demanded.

Grant drained his glass and took hers from her. 'No answer which you'd appreciate to that, except that most desirable things have their price, and I'd count Maracca among them. But if you wouldn't——' Turning her about, he made to walk her to the door, saying, 'Come along, it's time we went down and mingled.' But Fern halted in mid-floor and opened her bag, took out her wedding ring and handed it to him.

'I'm a spinster, remember,' she said. 'At least

all your women friends will expect to see me with a bare third finger, even if the men don't notice. So take it back, please. It doesn't signify what it did between us.'

She watched him slide the ring down to a first knuckle, which was as far as it would go. He said, 'Did it ever—to you?' then went over to the bureau and opened and closed a drawer on the ring dropped carelessly inside.

She didn't know what she had expected of her gesture. His outright anger? His sarcastic scorn? Even his pleading to her to keep the ring—beyond which her speculations were blank. What she hadn't foreseen was that he would treat it—his pledge to her!—as if it were a silly bauble from a chain store with no past meaning at all.

That defeated her. She went with him in silence out to the lift.

CHAPTER THREE

DURING the evening Fern was addressed by her maiden name so often that she could almost accept that it still belonged to her. In introducing her Grant used it easily, and Mrs Logan had spread the news so thoroughly that she had already met the Chief of Opal Oil's daughter that Fern found herself the centre of attention for far more people than whose own names and standing she could remember.

She was invited to picnics in the mountains of the interior, to tennis and swimming parties, to the races, to go fishing at night, to tour sugar, tea, banana plantations, and by contrast, to visit the temples of all the religions, Hindu, Moslem, Buddhist, Christian, which existed harmoniously side by side in Maracca.

She accepted and promised, suppressing a prick of conscience that she would be fêted under false pretences. Because that was Grant's fault, no responsibility of hers at all. And if he wanted to disown her as his wife, it seemed she could fill her engagement book quite adequately under her own steam!

Compared with her encounters with so many leisured, sophisticated people it was almost a relief to meet someone who was holding down an ordinary, everyday job. This happened when Fern, between dances, found herself sitting next

to a rather plain, angular young woman of about
thirty with no pretensions to elegance, but a voice
and manner which commanded attention when
she spoke. She announced to Fern abruptly, 'I'm
Rhoda Camell. I run the camp creche for Opal.
And you needn't bother to make the hoary joke
about my name, for I've heard it too often
before.'

Fern's lips formed the name and she smiled.
'I'll bet you have! I'm Fern Stirling.'

'I know. You were out at the plant this morning. Why didn't Grant bring you into the
creche?'

'He—Mr Wilder——'

'He likes to be called Grant.'

'Oh—— Well, he told me about the creche, but
perhaps he thought we hadn't time, as I had to
meet my father for lunch. I'd have liked to see it,
though. Do you run it alone? How many children
do you get?'

'With one girl helper and a boy for the cleaning.
Quite a crowd, usually. The European children
go to nursery school. The creche is for the
Maraccan women who can't leave their babies at
home when they come to work, in the canteen
and the Club and as office cleaners. Doc Croft
keeps an eye on them and does a clinic every week.
You fond of children?' Rhoda Camell shot the
question at Fern.

If only Grant had stayed with her, she might
have had a baby walking and talking by now, Fern
thought with a pang. 'Yes, very,' she told Rhoda.
'Especially tinies.'

'Then get Grant to bring you along some time.'

Rhoda got up to go. 'I'm leaving about now,' she said. 'I need beauty sleep more than most of you, and I have to be up at six, with the clients milling on the doorstep by half-past.'

Fern gasped. '*So* early—for such babies?'

Rhoda nodded. 'Maraccan working hours begin at sun-up. Everyone, including the office staff, is on the job by then.'

When Rhoda had left her Fern saw Grant across the floor. He came to her, tapping the glass of his watch. 'Close to midnight,' he said. 'A last turn before the show?'

She stood up and went to his arms for a conventional waltz. This had always been their perfection, which was why her imagination always shrank from the picture of him dancing with anyone else in the same way.

For his way had always been a kind of love-making to her, strangely at the same time a dominance of her and a surrender to her. They executed no extravagant movements, made no outward show of a unity of which they were both aware; dancing together they were able to achieve one vibrant entity, and there seemed no reason why, on a physical plane, they could not achieve it still. But they did not. Tonight there was nothing special between them, no sparking magic to draw them together. They were even able to chat as they danced, like polite strangers.

At least, Fern thought, she hadn't had to watch him with Rose de Mille, for she hadn't been on the dance-floor all the evening. When Fern mentioned her Grant said, 'She doesn't mix on Gala nights. She knows the value of "effecting an entrance". It's all part of her act as the complete professional.'

'How well do you know her?' queried Fern.

He slanted a glance down at her. 'I thought you'd never ask! It depends on what you mean by "well".'

'You know exactly what I mean,' Fern snapped. 'You seem to be fully abreast of her habits.'

Grant said, 'There was a time when I'd have said you and I knew all each other's habits. But I wouldn't claim now that we know each other well. Would you?'

It was no answer to her question and she realised she wasn't going to get one.

For the midnight floor-show there was first a magnificent display by Malaysian dancers in gorgeous silken robes and fantastic headdresses. The men mimed battle scenes and extravagant love-ardours to the point of suicide; the women moved coyly about the stage in steps so mincing and imperceptible beneath their robes that if their gliding hadn't taken them to another spot, it was scarcely credible that they had moved. Their very fingers had a language of their own, and the sinuous undulations of their bodies were in expressive contrast to the withdrawn impassivity of their Eastern faces.

The clamorous applause for them died down; the dais was darkened and Rose de Mille appeared at the back of it in an aureole of light. She was in a figure-fitting sheath of silver cloth from neck to wrist to ankles. The effect was of a glittering silver tube moving down to stand in the curve of the piano, after the merest dip of the auburn head in acknowledgment of its audience.

There was no order to Rose de Mille's choice of songs. They ranged from the gutter ditties of Piaf to contralto opera arias; from *Greensleeves* in English to *Lili Marlene* in German; from Grieg to Dvorak and to haunting *flamenco*. She sang on with little pause, and at the end she disappeared in her darkness and returned to give no encore.

Her departure marked the end of the evening and Fern and Grant joined the outgoing crowds. In the car Fern tried to analyse her feelings about Rose de Mille. They were a mixture of unstinted admiration of the woman's expertise, of the nag of not knowing what Grant was to her, and of the unwelcome realisation that in the matter of poise and worldly experience she herself was not in the same league.

Repelled by jealousy, drawn by curiosity, she asked Grant, 'Father is going to give a party in *Calypso* one night. Do you think Rose de Mille would come and sing?'

Grant laughed. 'I daresay—if she and the Chief saw eye to eye on the number of pennies she would want,' he said.

'Oh—I thought perhaps, as a friend of yours——'

'Which she is. But the labourer is worthy of his hire, and I'm not asking her to play performing seal for free.'

'I didn't *mean* for free,' Fern denied, not sure whether she had or not. She had just wanted a closer encounter with the enigma of Rose de Mille than she had had yet.

'All right, then, go ahead. Let Sir Manfred name his figure and Rose can please herself.'

'You make her sound very mercenary!'

'Just a working gal who doesn't need to sell herself down-market, that's all,' said Grant. Approving the woman, defending her. Keeping me guessing, thought Fern, no wiser by her ruse than before.

When they were through the town, instead of turning down to the docks Grant took the coast road in the opposite direction. It ran parallel to a long curve of beach bordered by wind-twisted palms, between which could be glimpsed the white-gold of the sands being teased by the frilly lace of surf at the water's edge.

'Where are you going?' Fern asked.

'Rounding off the evening in the accepted way.'

'Wh-what do you mean?'

'You must know.' He stopped the car and slid an arm across the back of her seat. 'How many times have you been driven home from parties in the last three years when you *haven't* expected to be kissed goodnight?'

She thought of all the butterfly pecks she had endured and had returned for politeness' sake. Her short laugh was mirthless. 'I—It doesn't follow. You don't——'

'Don't qualify as an escort? Or don't mean to exact my dues?'

Her heart began to thump. 'That was different. Just a way of saying thank you for the evening. You can't want to——'

His hand tightened round her shoulder. 'Can't I?' There was a deeper note in his voice. 'Why do you think I brought up the subject?'

'I don't know, unless to embarrass me.'

'As if the thought occurred!' he scoffed. 'Couldn't it be that I'm curious as to how much you've learned about kissing in the interval— whether too much or not enough? Come, let's see——'

Without an attempt at an embrace, he took her chin between finger and thumb and tilted it, as if to bring her face into a better light. Then he put his mouth to hers in a kiss that was no more than a teasing, provocative caress for her lips, gone hungrily eager at the passionless touch of his.

She found herself with no will to draw back from the tide of feeling which was betraying her to him while he remained unmoved. She craved for the vitalising magic which used to leap between them when they kissed, but while her whole body signalled its ache for him, he must be richly savouring an arousal of her which he had no intention of satisfying. His lips' leisurely exploration of cheek, ear-lobe, throat in soft, warm contact with her flesh was simply a playing with her, cat and mouse! The thought lent her the courage to draw back from him, panting for control. He did not try to hold her.

'Tch, tch, such abandon over a goodnight kiss!' he mocked. 'If I flattered myself, I could almost believe you'd missed my technique.'

More angry now than hurt, 'Don't flatter yourself, for you'd be wrong,' she retorted.

He pretended pained surprise. 'Mean to say you always get as hot as that for——?'

'Shut *up!*' she shouted, thumping the dashboard, hurting her fist. 'You didn't want to kiss me and I didn't want you to. It was simply your way of humiliating me, *showing off* how far apart we are, underlining how little I matter any more. As if I didn't know; as if you had to find out whether I can and do respond to other men, or whether your leaving me had turned me into a dried-up old prune, before you could accept how little *you* matter to *me* any more!' she finished in a rage.

Grant said equably, 'Well, thanks for small mercies. At least you don't claim that with a mere kiss—meant to tantalise, by the way—I'm trying to shackle you into matrimony again against your will. Which is just as well. For I'm not.'

Fern nodded tautly. 'Exactly. Just as well—because I wouldn't come. And now please take me back.'

Her father had gone to bed, but when she looked in on him he was waiting to hear how the evening had gone. She sat on the end of his bed. 'I met heaps of people and collected so many invitations that I'll have difficulty in fitting them all in,' she told him.

'I'm glad,' he approved. 'You feel compensated for anything you could be missing in London?'

'More than,' she smiled. 'Only——'

'What?'

'Well, now that I've made some contacts of my

own, do you expect me to go on depending on Grant to take me about?'

'Not if you'd rather not. We'll lay on a car and driver who can take us anywhere we want to go. I shall need one anyway. But I'm afraid you may still be meeting Grant quite often. As Freda Logan said, people here move in a pretty confined circle.'

'I'll risk that. As long as he can't make a favour of toting me around. As long as people don't start pairing the two of us in their minds. As long,' she concluded grimly, 'as I needn't hand him the chance to feel free to enjoy baiting me with the false situation he's put me in, that's all I ask.'

'He did that tonight? Embarrassed you? What makes you think he enjoyed doing it?'

'By the way he kept his cool when he'd driven me to lose mine. He took me up to his apartment before the Gala began. I reminded him that he'd turned me into a spinster again and handed him back my wedding ring. He took it, taunted me that it had never meant anything to me, and if there'd been a wastepaper basket handier than the drawer he put it into, I know he'd have thrown it into that.'

Sir Manfred sighed despairingly. 'You should be thankful that putting it out of sight in a safe place was all he did with it. He could well have been tempted to try to ram it down your throat. My dear girl,' Sir Manfred reached for her hand, 'can't you *realise* the affront to a man in having his ring returned?'

'The reason why I had to, why I couldn't go on

wearing it in public, was his doing, wasn't it?' Fern demanded.

' "Six of one and half a dozen of the other"—as I heard the story,' her father quoted. 'Anyway, if you couldn't bear the sight of it in your jewel-case you could have given the ring to me to care for. And should you need reminding, love, that you refused my offer to send you back to England, so saving you all this?'

She nodded. 'I know. I did refuse, and would again.'

'You needn't,' he urged. 'You can still go.'

She withdrew her hand from his, stood and turned away. 'No. I took it on and I'll see it through,' she said, and heard his murmured, 'That's my girl!' as the door closed upon her.

In her cabin before she slept she remembered the mood of glee in which she had determined to keep as close a tag on Grant as possible. But she hadn't known it was going to be like this—that in every encounter with him it would probably be she who would be retiring to lick her wounds, humiliated and powerless against his determination to hurt her. Nor had she deserved her father's praise of her bravado in 'seeing it through'. For that hadn't been courage speaking. It had been her effort to convince herself that, given the few weeks of her stay in Maracca, Grant's attitude must soften. He needed time, she argued. Before she went back to England he *must* admit the injustice to her of his masquerade, and Grant conceding his failure to bring her to heel was something she had to be there to see.

On the wishful thinking that it had to happen, she fell asleep.

The next morning Sir Manfred organised their chauffeured car, and suggested that if she had nothing else planned, she should drive with him out to the camp. Fern agreed, deciding to use Rhoda Camell's invitation to visit the creche. There, she felt pretty sure, she could spend a morning out of Grant's orbit!

The creche was a light airy hall not far from the main canteen. Arriving at the open door, Fern was met by a babel of children's voices speaking half a dozen languages including the local patois, and crying and laughing in an unidentifiable chorus. As Fern watched, a pretty Maraccan girl in her teens, neat in white apron and nurse's veil, came into the crowd, selected a tiny to tuck under each arm, disappeared with them into a row of cubicles, and returned for two more, irresistibly reminding Fern's sense of humour of a farmer's wife choosing braces of plump cockerels for the pot.

At a table covered with a cloth a young bearded man of about her own age was handing biscuits from a tin in one hand and pouring mugs of milk from a large jug in the other. Rhoda was nowhere to be seen.

As Fern moved forward the man looked round, put down tin and jug and came over to her. She held out her hand, smiling. 'Miss Camell invited me. I'm Fern Stirling,' she said.

Frank blue eyes under bushy blond brows smiled back. 'I know. I saw you at the Gala last night. I hoped I'd meet you, but—— Anyway, I'm

Ben Croftus, the medicine man around here. So sorry about Rhoda. She had to go into town to sort out a problem for one of the mothers and left me to hold the fort until she gets back. Won't be this morning, though. So may I show you round instead?'

'If you've time. You seem to be very busy,' Fern said.

'Nearly finished, and when Mahe has put down her babies for their rest, she can take over. Have you met Mahe yet?' Ben Croftus asked. 'No? Well, I won't interrupt her now. Rhoda will introduce you.'

'And I needn't stop you. I can come again another day,' Fern offered.

'That's all right. When the inmates are fed, I have a couple of babes to see and some prescriptions to write up. After that I'll be free, and the mothers call to collect the children at the noon siren. They only attend the creche in the mornings.'

'Could I do anything to help?' asked Fern.

'Why, yes, if you'd care to. You could finish serving the milk, and when they start drifting back to play, you could keep an eye on them until Mahe can take over. You like kids?' the doctor asked, refilling the milk jug and handing it to her.

'Very much,' she told him. 'Shall I take charge of the biscuits too?'

He left the job to her and disappeared towards the cubicles. An awed silence struck the tableful of children as Fern took over. Round dark eyes surveyed her, shy heads were lowered, and nobody seemed to want her wares. But once one bold spirit had pushed his mug forward, others did the same, and presently, warming to Fern's dumb show of smiles and gestures, the whole party was jabbering again. To her ears their English was too mixed with Maraccan patois for her to understand; their French was purer and she managed to chat with one or two of them in this. When they left the table she cleared it, and was helping to pat pies in the sandpit when first Mahe and then the doctor returned.

Mahe's smile for her was very sweet. 'The Mem will come again when Camell Mem is here?' she begged.

'I'd love to. I'll telephone beforehand next time,' Fern promised.

'Come and case the joint,' Ben Croftus invited her, and took her on a tour of the rest cubicles, the kitchens, his surgery and the amenities of the main hall—the climbing stands, the sandpit, the low work-benches and tiny chairs, a brightly coloured abacus and a piano. When she thanked him and was about to go, he said impulsively, 'My car is outside. Let me give you a drink at the Club before you have to meet Sir Manfred?'

'The Club? That's Le Corsair?'

'Yes, where we unmarrieds have our quarters.' He looked at his watch. 'It's not noon yet. There'll be a crowd in the bar after the siren has gone. But it'll be pretty quiet still. Do come.'

He wanted to tell her about himself, and over their long drinks on the Club verandah she let him.

He loved his job, his first since qualifying. He

meant to specialise in paediatrics, but he must put in a long stint in general practice first. He would hate to leave Maracca, but he couldn't afford to let it last too long; he must move on.

'How long have you been here?' Fern asked.

'Almost since Opal Oil came, and they needed an M.O. At first we camped in tents and my clinic was a wooden hut. But that's all of two years ago, and that must soon be enough in one place.' He paused to laugh selfconsciously. 'When I marry, my girl will have to like trailing me wherever I go. But if everything were right between us, she would want to, wouldn't she?'

The question was a little too near the knuckle for Fern's liking. 'It would depend on the girl, I think,' she evaded.

'Well, of course,' Ben agreed. 'But put it to yourself, for instance. If *your* man were a rolling stone, wouldn't you play along and like it?'

She got out of that one with a laugh. 'That's what's known as a hypothetical question,' she said.

Ben's blue eyes twinkled. 'In other words, one heck of an impertinence! O.K. But here's another for you to snub if you must—*Is* there a man for you in that way at present, Miss Stirling?'

'Fern, please.' She wanted to shiver whenever she heard her maiden name. She felt she wasn't lying when she said, 'At present, no.'

'Then it wasn't fair to ask you my hypothetical bit.' After a pause he said, 'But I'm glad I did.' And then, 'You came to the Gala with Grant Wilder. I suppose you and Sir Manfred know him well?'

'For a long time. But I didn't know he was out here until I arrived.'

At that Ben puzzled, 'But Sir Manfred would have——?'

'Oh yes, he knew the Opal Board had appointed Grant. It was only a surprise to me.' Feeling she might have to begin to lie in earnest, Fern looked at her watch. 'Thank you so much for the drink, but I must be going now. Will you drive me down to the main office to collect my father?'

'Sure thing.'

The siren had blared some minutes earlier, and as they left the bar a straggle of men came in. They greeted Fern's companion, 'Hey, Doc!' looked with curiosity at Fern, and a wolf whistle followed her out.

'Beaten the boys to it,' Ben Croftus chuckled. 'They don't so often get an eyeful of a lovely like you.' But he hadn't Fern's attention. Expecting only to visit the creche, she hadn't reckoned on encountering Grant. But he was approaching, had seen her and stopped. His glance from her to Ben was a question.

Ben explained for her. Grant told her, 'I didn't know you were coming over,' had a few words with Ben, and went on. Ben said, 'Grand chap, Wilder. We're lucky. Mows down the girls, but the feeling gets about lately that he's booked.'

'Booked?' Fern echoed.

Ben nodded. 'Rose de Mille—the star of last night's show.'

'Really?' said Fern, evincing no interest at all. It had occurred to her that seeing her with Ben, hearing they had had a drink together, would do Grant no harm. While he was preoccupied with his Rose de Mille, she might do worse than pretend to a conquest or two of her own. Flirtations with no serious futures intended had been easy enough in London. Why not here?

In her full days and nights which followed they were only too easy. She met Grant at parties, sometimes expecting to see him, sometimes not. But she no longer had to depend on him to escort her. If no one offered to call for her, Cristo their chauffeur took her, or when she and Sir Manfred were both invited, they went and returned together. It was very seldom that she lacked the company of some man with whom she had danced last night or would be meeting again at a swimming party tomorrow. Owing to the dawn to late afternoon hours worked, even at the oil camp, there was plenty of evening social life to be had, and plenty of eager people with whom to enjoy it. Though of course Ben's hours were not routine, whenever he was free he was not far from Fern's side; so often so that they began to be paired in the way that she had refused to be paired with Grant. 'Ben and Fern' became a unit to be invited, and Fern was so universally 'Fern' that she hadn't to cringe at the sound of 'Stirling'. Sometimes, she reminded herself longingly, to be Fern Wilder once more. But the memory of that carelessly abandoned wedding ring in Grant's drawer could always harden her spirit again.

Sir Manfred gave several small dinner and lunch parties on board *Calypso*, and planned a

more ambitious affair for an evening about ten
days before his and Fern's planned return to
England. All the executive personnel of Opal were
invited, as were high-ranking members of the
island's parliament, and the many friends Fern
had made. The yacht was dressed overall for the
occasion; tactfully approached by Sir Manfred,
Rose de Mille was to sing to the company after
dinner; Sir Manfred meant it as the ultimate in
salutes from his Company to Maracca for its hos-
pitality, and to judge by the number of accept-
ances, Maracca responded with enthusiasm.

Fern dressed for the evening in jacaranda-blue
Indian silk, bought in Port Dauphin and
fashioned for her by the incredible skill of a
Chinese seamstress. It fell in soft draperies to her
silver-sandalled feet, and she caught back her hair
under a twisted rope of silver filigree from Port
Dauphin's oriental market. On her shoulder she
pinned an orchid, its petals tipped with blue, the
gift of her dinner partner-to-be, the French
Maraccan Mayor of the city. Sir Manfred would
partner his wife; Grant would escort the wife of
the First Minister; Rose de Mille, according to
her custom, preferred not to dine before singing,
and was allotted a cabin as her dressing-room.
From there she sent a message, asking to see
Fern.

Fern found her lying down, wearing a peignoir
and with astringent-soaked pads over her eyes.
Without rising or removing the pads she offered a
graceful hand to Fern and murmured, 'So kind of
you to indulge me in eating nothing before an
engagement. Afterwards, just a glass of cham-

pagne and a wafer of sandwich—it would be possible to arrange that?'

'Of course,' Fern assured her. 'Is there anything you need now?'

'Nothing, thank you. Everything goes well?'

'I think so. I hope so.'

'And you? You are dressed? Yes? Then this I must see——' Still lying flat, Rose whipped off the pads and appraised Fern through liquid brown eyes. 'Ah,' she approved, 'that is just your colour—and style. Grant, partnering you, is going to be the envy of all the other men!'

Fern said, 'Oh, I'm not going in to dinner with Grant Wilder. We've paired him with Madame Desmarais, and I'm being escorted by the Mayor.'

The other woman's lips pouted a moue of distaste. 'Too bad for you. But of course protocol must be served, even though it separates lovers— But tell me, you have not been seen often in Grant's company lately? Close friends in England, I understood from him? But here? You have found other company which you prefer?'

'I've certainly met a great many people who've been generous enough to invite me to all kinds of things and to take me about,' Fern said guardedly.

'Ah! With one or two of the men your favourites, no doubt? For example, the oil camp's handsome young bearded doctor? Hasn't one heard——?'

Whatever the hint behind that, Rose did not complete it, but replaced her eye pads while Fern thought that, for all her aloof air, she seemed to be alert enough to island gossip which Fern had no wish to satisfy. She murmured instead, 'You can't think how we're all looking forward to your recital'—a tribute which, without taking her blind gaze from the ceiling, Rose accepted with a faint smile and a wave of her graceful hand.

'It is always so pleasant to be appreciated for one's art,' she said. 'Just as it is to be complimented by a man on whatever poor attraction one may have as a woman. Most Englishmen I have met are so very gauche at it. But there are exceptions. Grant Wilder, for one . . . He has such flair for making one feel one *is* a woman—and desirable. Some time, Miss Stirling, you should coax him into flattering you, however airily. You would find it a delicious experience!'

As Fern closed the cabin door behind her, her lips framed a silent uncomplimentary word to describe Rose de Mille.

After the formalities of dinner for the V.I.P.s and when Rose had given her perfectly chosen recital and retired with her accompanist, the mood of the evening relaxed. People abandoned their dinner partners for company they preferred; there was dancing, the bar was busy, and couples disappeared into and reappeared from the shadowed places of the decks and corridors.

Finding herself alone and needing air, Fern strolled out on to the starboard deck, not knowing that she had been seen and followed, until there was a touch on her shoulder and she found Ben leaning elbow to elbow with her on the deck-rail.

'You've been keeping your distance all the evening,' he accused her.

'Not guilty. You've been keeping yours,' she smiled.

'Not guilty either. It's been kept for us by the hordes of Sir Manfred's guests. Boy, what a party! Maracca will be talking about it for years to come.'

'I'm glad it's been a success. It's meant a lot to Father to show the Opal flag. How long do you think people will be staying now?' Fern asked.

Ben nudged her gently. 'Hey, the night is yet young!' he chided. 'That sounded as if you wanted to be rid of us. But surely not yet? Come on, let's look at the view for a while, and don't try to tell me that you and Sir Manfred didn't lay that on too!'

She knew when his arm went round her shoulders, and that it was pleasant to feel it there. They looked out over the harbour to seaward, the water a dark unruffled silk except for the spread floor of colour cast by *Calypso*'s lights and the lesser reflected twinkles from the other craft at their berths. Ben murmured, 'Imagine setting out on a sea like that, setting out for—well, anywhere new, with your chosen girl at your side, going along too. Venturing together—wherever, what would it matter? Just give me time—a year or two here, a couple more there, and the right girl, and I'll *make* it happen, you'll see!'

Fern knew when his hold tightened; knew that when he turned her to him he was going to kiss her; knew that she was going to let him, for the sheer comfort of feeling herself wanted, if only in the person of that shadowy girl in Ben's future, who would go with him wherever he went, who wouldn't be at his side at all if he didn't know he could trust her there—his will, her will all the way . . .

Ben's kisses were a gentle homage to which she had no right, Fern knew. He had kissed her lightly before, but not, as now, seeking promises of her which she could not give. But her hunger for another man's passion betrayed her into a surface response which her spirit did not back, though it seemed to satisfy Ben as to its sincerity.

And it was so—she, submissive to Ben's ardent embrace—that Grant, strolling alone, came upon them. Fern thought that Ben did not realise he had passed by. But she did, and realised bleakly that her plan to stimulate him to jealousy of her flirtations was not going to work. If for no other reason, it must fail because her own heart could bring no enthusiasm to it. She withdrew from Ben's arms, her pretence of response to him quite dead.

A day or two later she kept what was planned to be her last date with a French couple and their young son and daughter, both on holiday from school in Paris.

She spent the day with them on Monsieur Arnau's tea-estate up country, and in the evening they joined another party for the rare spectacle of Western ballet by a visiting company from South Africa.

At the end of the evening Fern assured the others that Cristo would be collecting her, and they parted in the foyer. Port Dauphin's attractive small theatre had been packed for the perform-

ance, and Fern expected to have to wait for
Cristo to take the car's turn in the queue at the
entrance.

She stepped outside once or twice to see if he
were in sight, and it was on her third sally that
Grant's car drew up and, alighting, Grant came
to join her on the entrance steps.

He said, 'You're waiting for Cristo to meet
you?'

'Yes. He's late. Have you seen our car anywhere?'

'He won't be coming. I'm taking you back.
Come on——' his hand went beneath her elbow.
'We're holding people up.'

She resisted his grasp. 'You needn't. Cristo will
be along.'

But Grant was already propelling her to his car
and putting her into it. He drove away at speed,
nosed from the kerb by the next car behind him.

Fern puzzled, 'I don't understand—has
something happened to Cristo or the car? Does
Father know you're driving me back instead?'

'Yes. He countermanded Cristo and asked me
to.'

'Why?'

Grant shrugged. 'Did you have a good evening?
How was the ballet?'

'Lovely. Have you seen it?'

'Yes. I took Rose on Sunday, when she doesn't
sing at the Meurice.'

As he spoke Grant was swinging on to the
quayside, silent and deserted at that time of night.
The vessels alongside loomed darkly; there was
the length of three to pass before *Calypso*'s berth.

But what——? Fern sat up abruptly, staring. Beyond the third ship there was only emptily lapping water.

Calypso had gone.

CHAPTER FOUR

IT was impossible! It couldn't be true! There had to be some explanation which would make nonsense of her bewildered fears—*had* to be! During the day, for some nautical reason she didn't understand, *Calypso* must have been moved to some other berth. Yes, that was it. Simple, if surprising. Yet why hadn't Grant told her so? Why, of all sinister things, had he driven straight to this empty dock, stopped the car, switched off his engine, as if this were their journey's end?

Fern turned frightened, indignant eyes upon him. 'What's all this in aid of?' she demanded. 'Where's the yacht?'

'I'm afraid she's sailed,' he said.

'*Sailed?* She can't have! What do you mean—sailed? Where for?'

'England, ultimately.'

She felt a wild impulse to spring at his throat. 'Don't *joke* with me!' she rasped. 'Father wouldn't—— We aren't due to leave for another week. What about me? I know you can't be serious, but if by an outside chance you are—*what about me?*'

Grant said levelly, 'Yes, what about you? Typical, but understandable, I suppose, that in any dilemma the first concern for Fern Stirling should be for herself. And so——'

A bolt of dread shot through her. 'You mean

Father *has* gone? Suddenly like this, because he's ill or something? Or something awful has happened at Head Office? Or—tell me?'

Grant shook his head. 'Nothing like that at all. Simply your father's considered decision to go back to England without you.'

'He—he's been thinking about it, deciding to, without telling me?'

'Reluctantly, yes.'

'But why?'

'Two main reasons. The first, we've disappointed him, you and I. He'd banked on Maracca's selling you the idea that you might come to terms with accompanying me wherever I'm sent by Opal, and he was hoping that almost the mere sight of you would persuade me to take you back. And neither has worked. Then, reason two—with nothing solved by this flip, he's been dreading returning you to the London scene for a renewal of the juvenile razzamatazz from which he had to prise you before. And so he saw the force of the argument that for the time being you should stay here.'

'Whose argument?' Fern pounced. 'Yours?'

'Debated between us. We kicked the idea around, battling with his conscience as well as the practicalities of leaving you here to face the facts of life without the backing of an influential and indulgent father. He had emotional misgivings about betraying your trust in him, and the practical one of there being nothing to stop your following him by the first available flight.'

'Which I could!'

'Given the necessary cash,' Grant pointed out.

'There's such a thing as credit. Heard of it?' she countered.

'Just about,' he agreed smoothly. 'But among other snags in our plan, we've dealt with that. You can't get enough credit on the moderate cash Sir Manfred has left for your immediate needs. Beyond that, he's opting out of any share in your keep, so that you will no longer enjoy the bonanza of running debit accounts to be settled by Daddy. I'm continuing the allowance I've always paid you, making that your sole income while you are here. And another thing—your father is putting more than distance between you and England. He's closing the house in Eaton Place and going out himself to the plant in Western Australia, and discouraging any but Opal communications.'

'M—making me your prisoner. Cutting off every way of escape. But what do you hope to gain by it—either of you?' Fern demanded.

Grant shrugged. 'I imagine he pins his faith to the workings of time.'

'And you?'

'I? I'm no such optimist. I merely co-operate.'

'I don't believe you. You don't want me here, but you can't resist the chance to punish me for being as I am, which I can't help. *You* are banking on time too. You think I shall get tired of this silly charade and give in. But I shan't.'

Grant murmured, 'The classic irresistible force against the immovable object—neither shall I.'

'Though I could get *very* tired of your playing cavalier to Rose de Mille, letting her suppose you're free, when you're not!'

Grant's brows lifted. 'Dog in the manger? For

shame! Poor Rose. I must warn her she's made an enemy for one of the usual pussycat reasons. As for punishing you, you could ponder the fact of there being harsher ways of punishing a deserting wife than by putting her under house arrest in exotic surroundings.'

'Just try anything harsher!' Fern warned through set teeth.

'Don't tempt me. I might go berserk without cause. Meanwhile——' he turned front again in his seat '——we have a minor problem or two to arrange——'

'Considerate of you to admit to problems,' she sneered. 'Dare I hope that it occurred to you that I should be left with only the clothes I'm wearing, and that I should have nowhere to sleep tonight?'

'You dare,' he confirmed. 'We thought of everything. Every feminine effect you had on board has been moved for safe keeping to my apartment, and a bed for the night awaits you there too.'

'Yours?'

'How did you guess?'

'Then you can keep it. I'll go to a hotel.'

'At this hour, with no personal luggage and on foot? For I won't drive you or sponsor you. I'm going home.'

'Home being where?'

'My apartment, of course. The camp club is run like the Y.M.C.A.—they close the doors at midnight. But the bed is yours. I can manage in the living-room, and the bedroom door has a lock. So do I take you there or not?'

Fern gave in. There were only a few hours left

of this calamitous night and she was sick of argument that got nowhere. But she could not resist a final barb. As Grant started the car, 'When you get the push from Opal, don't hesitate to come to me for references as to your flair for kidnap or blackmail, will you?' she taunted. At which Grant enraged her by touching an imaginary forelock. 'Thank you kindly, Mem,' he said. 'I'll remember that.'

He took her up to the penthouse floor through the hotel garage entrance, avoiding the foyer. Her cases were piled in his bedroom, where the bedclothes had been turned down on one side. She stood woodenly in the middle of the floor. 'What do you expect me to do now?' she asked.

'Go to bed, why not?'

'To sleep—after all this?'

'That was the idea in my giving up my bed to you. Would a nightcap help?'

'No,' she snapped.

'Then take your time. The bathroom is all yours. I'll go down for one at the all-night bar.'

When he had gone Fern sank wearily down on the bed. Obviously she couldn't stay in the things she had on, so she kicked off her evening sandals, stepped out of her long dress and decided on a quick shower before Grant came back. In his bathroom it was as if the three years of their separation hadn't happened. He had never taken to an electric razor and she recognised the smell of his shaving-soap; a pair of worn-down bedroom mules were those she had given him at their last Christmas together, and he still didn't squeeze his toothpaste from the bottom of the tube. Marriage was partly made of little signs of the loved one like that. Who now of the 'fringe benefits' of whom he had boasted shared their intimacy with him? she wondered—and fiercely dismissed the ache of nostalgia which had wondered.

In the bedroom again she looked out some day clothes for the morning—a morning for which, even if she could have slept, she had to stay awake and plan.

What was she to do? She must continue to take Grant's allowance. It was her legal right, and as he said, it would be her only income. But what proportion it was of the money she had been spending lately, and how far it would go to keep her in a hotel, she did not know. Certainly it wouldn't in a place of the quality of the Meurice, though it was in such luxury that her new friends would expect to find her, after they had swallowed the fiction that Sir Manfred had had unexpected calls to England which he had obeyed at too short notice to take her with him. Grant *must* back her up in this. He couldn't humiliate her by letting out the truth!

She slipped into a dressing-robe and lay down on the bed under the coverlet and sheet, listening for him to come back. When he did she pretended sleep lest he speak to her through the door. But there were only a few brief sounds of his moving about the living-room, and then silence.

Worry went on, with one dominant thought emerging. She would *not* be obliged to Grant for more help than had been forced on her tonight. She would show him and her father just how independent she could be, though how and where were questions to be solved before the night was out.

She did not know what time the hotel came to life, but when it did she had to be ready to walk out on Grant in some predetermined direction. But though she owed herself that gesture of defiance—what direction? Of all the many contacts she had made, she could think of no house on whose doorstep she could arrive uninvited for a stay of more than the hour or two of an ordinary surprise call. Real friendships took time, and she hadn't forged that kind yet . . . Or had she? One? She bit her lip, wondering. Perhaps there was somewhere she could go where even the earliest of arrivals wouldn't appear remarkable, since the place itself would be noisily alive by sun-up.

The oil-camp creche. She had kept that promise to Rhoda Camell to go back to it, and had been several times since, penetrating Rhoda's brusque manner to a point where she felt genuinely welcomed whenever she appeared. Even for Rhoda, the story of her father's precipitate departure would have to be discreetly edited, but she could trust Rhoda to evince no prying curiosity nor ask awkward questions. The creche was not a permanent haven, of course, but as a kind of staging-post Fern was glad she had thought of it.

Now, ways and means. She looked towards the morning, not caring at all for the prospect of Grant's taking her down to breakfast in the hotel or, almost worse, of his ordering it by room-service and of the waiter's finding her there with him. As if she were a common call-girl! Her gorge rose. No. She would insist on his taking her out by the back way they had come in—probably used for the same purpose before now!—Or, better still, she would leave herself before he woke up; leave a note to tell him she would send for her things.

But what hope had she of getting out? She threw back the sheet and tiptoed, barefoot, across to the door. By the dawnlight penetrating the shutters of the living-room she could make out Grant's humped body resting on two chairs. She daren't approach him; she stood listening to his measured breathing, then crept to the lobby shadowing the door to the back corridor and the service lift down to the garage yard which was open all hours.

She felt for the door handle, turned it. The door opened a crack. Not locked, then. So far, so good. If she could manage to dress and get through the routine again without——

She turned back. Across the archway between lobby and living-room a figure loomed—*Grant!*—and in the next instant he had lunged for her and pinioned her in his arms.

In his rough grip her short robe had fallen open. He was wearing a hip-length sashed jacket. Feet astride, his legs hard against hers, for long panting seconds they were body to body in an embrace which had nothing of love to it; only the passion of his anger and the shock of her enforced surrender to it.

'What do you think you're doing? Where are you going—in that?' he demanded thickly, with a flick at the lapel of her robe.

Fern pulled free of him and drew it around her.

'I couldn't sleep and I wanted to see if I could leave by that door as soon as I was dressed. I found it wasn't locked, and——'

'Of course it's not locked from this side. I gave you a bed for the night; I didn't put you behind bars. But—leaving at this hour? Where for? And what's your hurry?'

'I—meant to leave before you woke up, if I could,' she explained.

'With or without the courtesy of a note left for me under the clock? Why?'

'Because I can't bear to be under any more obligation to you, of course!' she retorted.

'Another hour or two of my irksome sponsorship, with breakfast thrown in—the very thought was anathema to you?' scoffed Grant.

She scorned to reply and turned away. But his hand on her shoulder swung her round to face him again.

'I wonder,' he said. And again, 'I wonder——'

'Wonder what?'

'Whether that's the real truth of this dawn foray of yours, barefoot, becomingly loosened hair, careless nudity? I ask myself—why, if you had to case the joint first, you didn't make one journey of it when you were dressed and ready to go? You must have guessed that, camped on two upright chairs, I wasn't likely to be deep in restful slumber, that there was at least a chance I'd hear you on this trip. And so——?'

Fern stared at him incredulously. 'I don't know what you're hinting at!' she claimed, though she feared she knew.

'Well, supposing your devious little mind

weren't hatching plans for escape at all, but perhaps was testing, to see if I could be tempted to re-explore the fascinations of a body I used to enjoy? Nothing too blatantly offered, of course. Just—dangled, as bait for the fool I'd be if I took it?'

She put her intuition into words. 'You're suggesting that I'd—I'd *stoop* to coaxing you into making love to me? Why on earth should I?'

'For petty satisfaction, perhaps. Perhaps as crafty means to an end.'

'*What* end?'

'Your hope that, if I were that kind of fool, I could ultimately be softened up to accept your terms for our future. But it's not on, my would-be Delilah. Lovely as you are, immediately handy as you are at the moment, and reluctant as I am to turn you down, you should be thankful that I'm boor enough to send you back to your chaste bed, none the worse for your gallant try to get me to share a romp in it with you. Come on—on your way. I could do with some more sleep myself.'

For that, for the unruffled irony behind the cruelly chosen words of insult, she struck him, and immediately found both her hands pinioned, while the scar of her open palm reddened his cheek. Angry, frustrated tears she could not wipe away blurred her sight as Grant picked her up bodily and carried her back to the bed. None too gently he laid her down, and she fumbled for a handkerchief, which he produced from the pocket of his robe. Looking down at her, he catalogued, 'All the melodramatic tricks—undress, discreet seduction, shocked virtue, common assault, tears—my dear, if you hadn't made your tactics so darned obvious, who knows that you mightn't have had me saying, "Why not?"!'

Fern struggled up, supported by her elbows. 'Grant——' she appealed in a strangled voice. But just calling his name could not convey the depth of her shame and despair, and he had shown he would not heed any words she found to say. His wilful contempt had turned too savagely against her.

The city was wide awake when they met in the hotel coffee-shop three hours later. She had asked Grant to have her things sent to the cloakroom, where she would have them collected later, and though she had been ready then to call a taxi, he insisted she have breakfast first.

This morning she had forced herself to don the masks of pride and reserve as meticulously as she had seen to the simple perfection of her toilette of navy sleeveless suit, immaculate white sandals, bag and stiff straw boater, and a careful unobtrusive make-up which was all her healthy skin needed to hide even the ravages of last night.

Last night hadn't happened, she told herself. With Grant, for as long as she had to be, she would be all ice, all self-possession, all disdain of the subject if he tried to refer to it, however obliquely.

He did not. He had other things to say, the first being, 'Where do you plan to go from here?'

She wished she need not tell him, but of course she had to. 'To the camp creche,' she said, and was gratified that his echo showed she had surprised him.

'The creche? Why there? Don't you need somewhere——?'

'To live?' she supplied. 'Yes, and I'm counting on Rhoda to advise me. We've become good friends, and I'm pretty sure she'll tell me somewhere I can afford while I look for a job.'

Again she had the satisfaction of his surprise. 'You're thinking of looking for a job? Here? That's impossible. Forget it,' he ruled.

'Why?' She calmly buttered a rusk.

'Because, for one thing, you are who you are—the Chief's daughter.'

'Exactly. A grass widow and a grass orphan rolled into one. All the more reason for earning my keep,' she agreed sweetly. 'Go on.'

'For another, you're trained for nothing. You couldn't hold down a job.'

'I don't know. I'm bi-lingual in French and English, and I'm learning some of the patois. I can even add and subtract on my fingers, given time. Languages . . . mathematics . . . let's see—what else?'

'*Nothing* else!' Grant cut in savagely. 'You'll forget this nonsense here and now. I gave Sir Manfred my word that you would live on your income from me, and you'll do just that and no more.'

'And supposing I can't? Supposing,' she mimicked a high plaintive whine, 'supposing it won't *run* to all the pretties I want; won't—what's the phrase?—"keep me in the state to which I'm accustomed"—what then?'

Grant mocked, 'Poor little rich girl, fallen on

hard times! Since a bit of penny-scraping independence for you was the object of the present exercise, your character might have benefited by having to cope. But you've so many friends that I'd say your social life need suffer hardly at all for want of as many pretties and privileges and escorts as you've enjoyed until now. Fringe benefits, you know. Your sex collects some valuable ones too.'

'If, as a working girl, I find time to enjoy them,' Fern returned in her ordinary tone. She stood up, pushed in her chair and opened her bag. 'How much do I owe you for my breakfast?'

He stood, crashing his chair, making his gritted expletive no answer. So she dropped some rupee notes on the table and left the coffee shop at his side.

'I need a taxi to drive me out to Opal,' she told the hall porter, half expecting that Grant would offer to take her, and feeling slightly affronted when he did not. That was his come-back to her defiance of him, she thought. And wondered, as her taxi drove away, why she felt so little triumph at having won that round.

The creche's morning was well on its clamorous way when she arrived there. Today Mahe was dispensing milk and biscuits and Rhoda was 'putting down' her babies. Ben Croftus was not there.

''Lo there' and 'See you soon' was Rhoda's hail and farewell to Fern until she had finished what she was doing, and Fern took her usual cue on her visits to find something that needed doing, and doing it. This morning, in an apron regarded as hers, she was clearing up the litter of paper, broken chalks, paint-smeared rags and spilt water on the low working tables, when Rhoda came over to her.

'Second time this week. What gives?' asked Rhoda's economy of speech.

'Nothing. I just want your advice—when you've got time. No hurry,' Fern used the same crisp idiom.

'Stay all morning? Or come back at siren time?'

'I'll stay if I may.'

'Oke.' Rhoda reached for a baby which had fallen flat in the sand-pit, wiped sand from its nose and mouth, set it upright again and put a wooden spade in its hand before it had gathered itself to cry. Then she disappeared.

She had news for Fern at the end of the morning when the mothers had collected their children and unwonted quiet descended on the creche building. 'I'm losing Mahe,' she announced. 'She's going to be married next week.'

'Good heavens, she only looks about thirteen,' exclaimed Fern.

'Maraccan Buddhists marry young, in a ceremony that's only a blessing of the couple's house and a pouring of blessed water over their joined hands by their witnesses. No priest, no pledges. But it seems to work as well as ours, on the whole.'

'You're going to miss her. She's so sweet with the children,' Fern sympathised.

Rhoda nodded. 'Yep. Trained her myself to nursery-nurse standard. Now it's got to be done all over again, and raw material none too easy to find.'

'I suppose——' Fern looked at the idea which had struck her, and discarded it.

'Go ahead,' Rhoda invited. 'You suppose what?'

'Nothing. That is, you do want to train another young girl? Someone older wouldn't do?'

'I might. It depends. Why, got anyone in view?'

With a feeling of burning her boats Fern said, 'Yes. Me.'

At least Rhoda didn't laugh at her. 'Eight-hour-plus day, morning call six a.m., on duty six-thirty sharp? Forget it,' she said.

'No, I'm serious. Listen,' Fern begged. 'Things have——have sort of changed. My father has had to go back to England and then to Australia without me. Which leaves me here a bit indefinitely, and——and I want something to do.'

'Why?' asked Rhoda unhelpfully.

'To fill in my time. To feel I'm of some use, and I think I could be, here.'

'H'm. Were you holding down a job in England?'

'No. There wasn't any need for me to work, and there was a lot of playing going on all the time in my circle.'

'No need to work and a lot of playing to do—same here too, surely? But suddenly you want to be "of use". I wonder why?' Rhoda pondered this to Fern's embarrassment, then shook her head. 'Sorry, it's not on. For one thing, you wouldn't be "of use" to me, until I'd taught you your job. All household and child-care chores.'

'You say you must teach someone,' Fern

whipped back. 'And I do help a bit, don't I, when I come?'

'In a Lady Bountiful way, taking round soup to the parishioners, yes, quite a lot, and we get on together, and I'd say you're teachable——'

'Thank you kindly,' Fern murmured.

'But for another thing of many, if your *Calypso* has sailed out on you, where do you propose to live? At a hotel? Anywhere in the city? And keep a dawn deadline here morning after morning? See the point, do you?'

Fern saw it. 'You mean you wouldn't trust me to do it from the city? Well, I don't have to live in Port Dauphin. Could I get lodging somewhere on the camp? How does Mahe come to work?'

'Walks six miles each way from her village. Not the same thing at all. Maybe you could get rooms in one of the staff bungalows. Or——' Rhoda paused for thought '——there's the annexe to my own bungalow next door; a room and a bathroom and a separate entrance. It's meant as a kind of ward in case we have to isolate a child in a hurry. But that's an outside chance. Yes, better have that if you're serious about coming.'

'Then you'll take me on? What about the rent?' Fern asked.

'Nothing. It's part of the creche premises, and you'll turn out the minute it's needed, if it is. You'll be paid by Opal, like Ben Croftus and me.'

'The Opal office here could turn me down if it thought fit?' Fern suggested, foreseeing Grant's ability to veto the plan.

'Could, but it won't, if I say I need you. When could you start?'

'If I brought my things out this afternoon, I could begin tomorrow.'

'Do that, then.' But Rhoda, who, to Fern's relief, had accepted her story at its face value remarkably well, had one searching question to ask. 'Do you see this idea as a kind of debutantes' pre-marriage domestic course?' she queried.

Fern coloured. 'What do you mean? What's the connection?'

'This social butterfly's sudden need to "be of use". Of use to a man, a particular man, that usually means. Hoping-to-be-engaged girls get the urge quite badly, I've noticed. But not you?'

Fern shook her head. 'Not me,' she confirmed. To be able to do an 'I told you so' at Grant was all the satisfaction she asked.

'My mistake. Only wondered if your nesting instinct was going into action and whether I knew the man,' said Rhoda.

CHAPTER FIVE

DURING the days which followed Fern was to question whether she would ever willingly accept the tyranny of the alarm clock. However early she went to bed, the night seemed to have only just begun when it was rudely jerked into morning again by the insistent shrill of that wretched clock. She had to force upon herself a rule to be out of bed and under a cold shower before it stopped shouting, or she wouldn't have waked properly at all.

By half-past six most of the creche's clients had been left there by their mothers, sisters or grannies, on their way to their own work of office cleaning or in the canteen and the Club. The nursery routine got under way with a cleanliness inspection of chubby hands; bibs had to be tied round necks and bodies hoisted into chairs round the communal table for a breakfast of milk and rice for the older children and warmed cereal feeds for the tinies.

After that there was some competition for the job of helping to clear away and wash up, while everyone else scattered for a period of free play—a noisy session of will-clashing rivalries and exhibitionism which taxed supervision to its utmost. That was followed by a 'quiet time'—in theory, when everyone was encouraged to settle to some sedentary task—but which in fact was 'quiet' only by comparison with the tumult which had gone before it.

There was always some mending, of toys or torn clothes, to do; first aid for cut fingers and grazed knees, baby-sitting with the smallest at their morning rest time in bed, feeding the perennially hungry and, it seemed to Fern, a continual keeping of the peace between these self-important little examples of the different cultures, Chinese, Indian, European and Arabic, which met and lived in reasonable harmony at the exotic cross-roads of Maracca.

Fortunately Fern discovered that, like Mahe, whom the children were going to miss, she had a certain talent for patching up quarrels and smoothing ruffled feathers. She supposed it was because she remembered her own childhood woes well enough to know what hurt the pride and outraged the senses, and was able to see justice done with a turn of humour which earned Rhoda's praise of her as a veritable King Solomon for the settling of disputes.

Into most mornings also were packed singing games and marching and the final lunch, as well as Ben Croftus's weekly clinic and his intermittent calls. Their charges were collected at noon, but for Rhoda and Fern there was still clearing up and preparation for the next day; sometimes they ate their midday meal together, sometimes one or other went to the canteen; other people's siesta time was usually far spent before Fern was free to take her own. After a rest in the shuttered cool of her room she often went for a swim in the camp pool at a quiet hour when the young mothers in the staff bungalows were putting their children to bed and their men were enjoying their sundowners at the Club bar. She spent most of those first evenings with Rhoda or in her room. Rhoda had Grant's formal sanction to employ her as crèche assistant, but he made no move to see her. Her main source of news was Ben who, though he heard and reported the general reaction to her sudden leap out of the social limelight, had the grace himself to respect her reserves about it.

He was frank with her that she had puzzled more people than she had pleased.

'It's a nine days' wonder. To hear some of them, you'd think you'd retired into a nunnery, and they'd give their right ears to know why. Someone—Freda Logan, in fact, poisonous woman—suggested in my hearing that it was a publicity gimmick—Daughter of Opal Chief goes slumming, something like that. Slumming, I ask you! of our bunch of mums and babes, as charming and decent a lot as you could find. Of course there are the real folks who give you full marks, but honestly, Fern, I think you should kill the nunnery idea stone dead. Do some more mingling. Show them you're still around and just as with it as ever.'

'I don't have the time now,' she pointed out.

'You have evenings; as much and more than I can ever be sure of having. Look—Grant Wilder's throwing an informal do at the Club tomorrow night. Or did you know? Has he asked you? No? Well, it's just a few of the fellows and their girls for drinks and gossip. Now you can manage *that*. Will you come with me?'

She had no reason for refusing. She had to meet Grant again some time, and in a crowd and in Ben's company, he could hardly snub her to her face. 'Thanks. I'd like to come,' she told Ben.

She had misgivings, however, when she and Ben joined the party on the Club verandah by the light of storm lanterns and candles in sconces hung from the bamboo roof. If Grant chose, he could make it chillingly clear that she was an unwelcome guest, which would puzzle and reflect upon Ben for bringing her. But when his raised hand in greeting to Ben included her, she realised she should have known better of Grant's public manners. Whatever his harsh judgment of her, it would be kept for her private hearing.

The party took its usual way of talk and drinks and arrivals and departures. Most of Grant's guests were his colleagues on the camp, and with them Fern found she was already accepted as 'one of us' and was drawn in easily to the camp gossip. She had begun to feel completely relaxed and at ease when Freda Logan, whom she had hoped to avoid, detached herself from another group and came over to her.

'You haven't been seen among the bright lights lately,' Freda said. 'People in your crowd are beginning to wonder what they can have done to offend.' Her little laugh made a joke of that, but Fern knew it for a joke with a sting.

'Just because I thought I'd like a part-time job after my father left?—what nonsense!' she scoffed. 'Nobody could think anything of the sort.'

'Yes, well—it was all so sudden,' Freda fenced. 'There was the Chief, here one day and gone the next, and the same day you'd flown to Good Works and camp living and haven't been visible since.'

'I had to live somewhere, and here, on the job itself, with Rhoda Camell, seemed the best idea,' Fern pointed out.

'But why the job? And such a job——! Nurserymaiding to a lot of little locals, no less. Why, if you were as bored as all that, you could have had anything open to you. Austin could have pulled strings. In fact, he would have taken you on as his own secretary, if you'd asked.'

'When I can't type, and I couldn't keep a filing system for peanuts? Besides, in six weeks I'd seen only one side of Maraccan life, and mixing with Maraccans themselves, as I do now in the creche, seemed as good a way as any of seeing another,' Fern claimed.

'Though why should you be concerned with Maraccans, when you're only visiting here, not permanently? Unless of course you're thinking of marrying here, which would explain a lot,' Freda Logan insinuated.

'Would it? A lot of what?' Fern's light tone hid her irritation at the catechism.

'A lot of people's guesses about you, of course,' Freda said sharply. 'About the various men you've been about with here, about which of them you might have your eye upon, if you've a taste for settling in Maracca. My dear, there are rumours enough flying round about you to fill a gossip column! I've even heard it said that you'd regard Grant Wilder as quite a prize packet, tagged *Manager, Opal Oil, Maracca*, now that he's persuaded Sir Manfred to give Austin the push!'

So that was it, thought Fern. Freda Logan's spite was an offshoot of her jealousy of Grant. Ironic, that she should thrust Fern on to Grant's side, in order to stress an enmity with which Fern had nothing to do! Fern could imagine his biting comment on that if he knew. For herself she could only retort with the cool sarcasm that she was flattered to have attracted so much notice, trusting that her enemy—and Grant's—would take the point that she was indifferent to anything her detractors said.

The party had been going for about an hour and she and Ben were in a group which Grant had just joined, when one of the Club's boys came to call Ben to the telephone.

Ben came back, crestfallen and apologetic. 'There's a thing! Emergency call to a heart case— a young chap, but it's his second attack, and I must get him into Port Dauphin hospital,' he told Fern. 'Wretched nuisance, having to leave now, but I may not get back, you see.'

Fern put down her glass. 'It doesn't matter. I'll come now, if you can drop me off at the creche?'

'Sure thing,' began Ben to a chorus of 'She doesn't have to go' and 'We'll see her safe, man,' above which Grant's incisive voice said, 'I'll see Fern home myself,' and someone put Fern's glass back into her hand.

As Grant had said, the Club kept modest hours, and the party broke up before midnight, by which time Ben had not reappeared. People drifted away by twos and threes, on foot and by car, leaving Fern and Grant, as host, till last.

At night the camp site had a silent magic all its own. In the yards and about the sheds and around the derricks nothing stirred in evidence of the churning activity deep underground which continued day and night. At ground level the darkness was the more intense by contrast with the great fans of spectrum-coloured flame which flared into the night sky from the mouths of the platformed columns known as cracking towers to the professionals. To Fern's lay imagination they looked like witches' cauldrons.

The night air was as warm as a summer's day, and Grant suggested they walk to the creche. On the way he asked whom she had talked to during the evening, and she told him, describing some of the people whose names she hadn't caught, omitting any mention of Mrs Logan.

At the door to her annexe she took her key from her bag and offered him her hand. 'Thank you for bringing me home,' she said.

He ignored her hand. 'I'll see you in.' He took the key from her and used it, standing aside for her to go in ahead of him, and closing the door behind him.

She switched on the light, as nervous of him as of a stranger. Remembering the Club hours she said, 'You mustn't stay. You'll get yourself locked out.'

'No. I had a word with Fadal, the boy on the door,' he said carelessly. He studied the austerity of the little room. 'So this is how the other half lives. Primitive but neat,' he commented.

'I didn't invite you to patronise it. It suits me,' Fern retorted, finding her spirit.

'Making the best of a bad job, or savouring the privileges of a career girl—your own latch-key, freedom to come and go as you please, without even a courtesy obligation to anyone, and the opportunity of entertaining your friends without question, to any hour of the night?'

Fern said, 'I'm enjoying my job and the convenience of living over the shop, as it were. I don't entertain. I think Rhoda would have something to say if I threw parties, and as you can see, there's no room and not enough chairs for more than a couple of people at a time.'

'*One* at a time could find somewhere to sit. If Ben Croftus had brought you home, would you have invited him to stay the night?'

She just contained a gasp, realising he was deliberately goading her to explosion, and determining not to gratify him. 'You've brought me home. Are you expecting me to invite *you* to stay the night?' she countered icily.

He mimicked an engineer speaking into a microphone. 'Just testing, testing. But no. You'd lose too much face if I refused, and if I accepted, you'd lose even more if you let me stay. No, you wouldn't risk it.'

'As long as you realise it was no more in my mind to invite Ben than to invite you,' Fern retorted. She shrugged her wrap from her shoulders. 'Will you go now, please? I have to be up early in the morning.'

He levered himself from the chair-back against which he had been leaning. 'On a job which couldn't have been more happily arranged for your purpose, could it?' he hinted.

'For my—purpose?'

'My dear, surely? The day-by-day propinquity! The opportunities for the intimate moment! The continual titillation of the poor chap by having you around——'

'You're talking about Ben?'

Grant's brows lifted. 'Who else? Keeping his homage by sharing his work with him, exchanging medical jargon between romantic hassles—oh yes, you laid your plans very well indeed!'

Aghast at his meaning, 'You're accusing me of having *angled* for this job because of Ben?'

'Well, didn't you? But don't belabour a confession. I've said it all for you. Congratulations— you didn't miss a trick.'

'You're the boss,' she snapped. 'If you thought that of me why did you let Rhoda take me on?'

'Ah, perhaps I didn't see through your motives at first, and when I did, I decided to give you enough rope to hang yourself. Because there's no future in grappling Ben's devotion, you know. He and I are two of a kind, rolling stones, both of us, and when the yen takes him to up stakes and move on, however deep his involvement with the current girl, she'll have to go with him—or else. At least, that's how I read his code about women.'

'Yes, so do I,' said Fern evenly.

'You've been warned, have you?'

'I don't need warning. I'm not "deeply involved" with Ben Croftus.'

'Nor he with you? You could have fooled me. I'd have said he's at the point of seeing your seduction just one move ahead.'

'Then if you think he's in danger of an affair

with me that's not on, shouldn't you warn *him*, not me?'

Grant turned at the door, his hand on the latch. 'And reveal a vested interest in you which I've kept dark so far? No——' he laughed unkindly, 'if you're only amusing yourself with him to pass the time, Ben must take whatever luck is in store for him.'

'Then it's nothing to you if I go on seeing him as I please?' Fern queried.

Grant laughed again. 'My dear wife-that-was, if in the future it means "anything" to me that you've gone, or want to go, too far with another man, you can be very sure you won't enjoy the consequences.'

He hadn't been laughing as he finished. His tone held threat. Then he opened the door; he was silhouetted against the night sky for a moment before the door slammed behind him.

What had he meant? Was he threatening divorce? Would he let their rift come to that in the end? Fern wondered what she had expected or hoped he would reply to her question. And remembered his implied doubt of his ability to care. And wanted to weep for sheer desolation and the vivid memory of kisses which used to set her afire.

That party of Grant's was the first of her excursions back into circulation, and soon she was accepting invitations for two or three evenings a week. Freda Logan's snide remarks about her disappearance were part of her motivation; the rest was the outcome of a defiant pride which needed to show Grant that her isolation had been self-chosen, not rejection by her friends, and a need to conceal from Sir Manfred that either her spirit or her will had been weakened by his defection. She ignored Grant's discouragement of communicating with him in Australia, and she wrote fully and graphically to him there, making much of the good times she was still having and the pleasure she got from her job. The manner of his leaving her and Grant's part in it she did not mention at all. She would *not* whine!

She was hearing more gossip now than ever percolated to the creche. She was again in the audience for all the sporting and business and romantic comings and goings of the island; inevitably she was kept informed of how frequently Rose de Mille and Grant were to be seen together—at the races, at the casino, Rose as a spectator when he was competing in water-ski events. Though Fern knew better and was tempted to hint so, there seemed no doubt in the public mind that they were unofficially engaged, and they were everywhere invited together, reminding Fern of her own rebellion against being paired with Grant when she had a good choice of other escorts. She had some still and, when he was free, always Ben. But it would have done much for her ego if Grant had chosen her instead of Rose for just one date. She would turn him down, of course. But she would have liked to feel she was somewhere in the running . . .

It was Ben from whom she heard of the growing rivalry between Austin Logan and Grant. Grant had been sent to Opal Maracca as the installation

manager of the projected offshore operation as
well as his supplanting of Logan in the directing
of the land-based plant. Fern remembered that
Sir Manfred had argued that, since some of the
personnel must be common to both schemes,
they must be under a common management—
notably Grant's, since Logan had no experience
in offshore structures. This arrangement was seen
increasingly sourly by Logan, Ben reported, and
now that the tow-out and the placement of the
first platforms was under way, Logan was being
as obstructive as his position allowed.

'He's telling Grant continually he can't spare
the men Grant needs, and though Grant has the
authority to requisition them, Austin isn't above
making trouble farther afield, among the men
themselves, persuading them that they must
watch out for their extra rights—danger pay and
so on, or Opal may cheat them, and in any organ-
isation of this size, there are always enough mal-
contents to listen.'

'What can Grant do about it?' asked Fern.

'Pull his rank. Offer firm contracts to cover
danger money, overtime hours, the lot. But with
Logan doing underground hinting that contracts
are only worth the paper they're written on, he
can't rely on the will of the men, and that's important.'

'Could he supplant Austin Logan?'

'Not from his present job as Grant's second-in-
command without Opal's authority, and Grant,
being the chap he is, wouldn't appeal for it, as an
admission that he can't manage his own ship. He
can, of course, and will, but meanwhile he has the

other half of the Logan pair to deal with as well.'

'Freda Logan? Well, I realised as soon as I arrived that she resented Grant. My father knew it too,' said Fern. 'But there's nothing she can do to influence the men, surely?'

'Not directly,' Ben allowed. 'Less so than Austin can, but she can do a lot with her subtle tongue, as you should know.'

Fern did, though she didn't relate to Ben the other woman's latest theories about her own supposed ambitions. They were hideously wrong and of only nuisance value, except as part of the pattern of intrigue against Grant. That, however, was important, and though her loyalty had to agree with Ben that Grant could handle it, she saw no harm in touching upon its developments in her letter to Sir Manfred, making of it a piece of gossip and foreseeing none of its consequences until they were upon her.

She had had no reply to her letter when she was surprised by an invitation to dinner from Grant. Rhoda answered the clinic telephone and called her to it. 'The Boss Man—for you. What have you been up to?' Rhoda wanted to know.

Grant said, 'Will you dine with me tonight? I'll call for you at eight.'

Fern remembered her resolve to refuse him and she hesitated. 'I'm not sure if I——'

'Nonsense. I'm not asking you for weeks ahead. You must know if you're free this evening. Are you?' he cut in.

'So far, yes. But there was a possibility——'

'Disregard it if it happens. I have to see you about something, and it won't wait. Don't dress—

we're going out of town. I'll see you at eight.' He rang off, leaving her to a whirl of nervous speculation as to what he could want of her so urgently. By the time she kept her date with him she had ranged from the wildly wishful thinking that he wanted to discuss a reunion on her terms, to the dark dread of the worst which could befall her—his request for a divorce. Any reason for urgency between these extremes escaped her.

She wore a pale green pleated dress with a matching cape and knotted a silk scarf with streaming ends round her hair. Grant was equally informal in short-sleeved shirt and slacks. Sitting beside him in the open car, gently teased by the soft night air, it became easier to think herself into the spirit of a pleasant evening outing. Over dinner in some little retreat in the hills or by the sea, nothing too terrible could be in store for her—could it?

It seemed that nothing was—at least of such urgency that it couldn't wait until after they had dined. On that drive into the country and over that meal on a quiet candlelit terrace of a lagoonside hotel, she deluded herself that time had rolled back for her and Grant. He was attentive and at his most debonair. Just so, on summer nights in London they might have driven down to the riverside to dine and to go back after midnight to sleep in each other's arms.

That had been when their wills and their bodies had moved to the same beat. Tonight, when they parted, she would sleep alone, and wished she could know for certain that, after this isolated evening with her, Grant would be doing the same.

In the end, when they had finished their coffee and all she could see of him in the darkness was the curling smoke of his cheroot, she grasped the nettle herself.

'You said there was something you had to say to me or tell me?' she reminded him.

The cheroot was held away from him. 'There was,' he said. 'There is. I thought we might enjoy our dinner first.'

'Then it's something I shan't like?'

'Something I'd rather not have to say.' He paused. 'You've written to your father. Have you had a reply?'

'Not yet.' Alarm for Sir Manfred caught at her throat. 'Why? What——?'

'He's phoned me. Wants to know the truth behind your inconsequential tattlings, and *I'd* like to hear what right you think you have to make gossip of Opal affairs which are of no possible concern to you?' Grant paused again. 'I'm referring, of course, to your report that we've internal trouble here, fostered by the Logans, implying that it could get out of hand. You don't deny passing on this extravagant nonsense, I'm sure. You'll remember having made news of it to your father?'

From pleasant dinner companion he had turned prosecuting counsel. Adjusting with difficulty, Fern began, 'I certainly did mention to Father what I'd heard——'

'From whom?'

She spread a hand and shrugged. 'From all over. From Ben Croftus.'

'In whom, as a professional type, one

should look for more discretion,' Grant ruled acidly.

Fern defended Ben. 'He *is* discreet in his own profession. And trouble with Austin Logan could be no news to my father. You and he have talked about it in my hearing.'

'Not as the ongoing fact you prattlers have made of it. And even it were that, whose is the major headache, do you suppose? Whose sole responsibility to deal with it?'

She knew the answer he expected. 'Yours, of course,' she said.

'Exactly. And when Opal Oil, Maracca, is in danger I can't handle, that'll be the day for an official report to Headquarters. Until then we aren't interested in rumour, slander, libel—the lot. Understood?'

Fern bowed her head. 'Though I think you could have put it more courteously.'

'Calumny is too ugly a subject for kid-glove treatment. You're an employee of Opal, and to have had you on the carpet in my office might have been even less courteous, mightn't it?' he queried.

'Yes,' she said. 'Thank you.' (For her dinner—the sugar on the pill of a warning he must agree she didn't deserve if she could report Freda Logan verbatim?) She was dispiritedly aware of anticlimax. She had come, braced for some settlement—one way or the other—of their personal issues. Yet all he was concerned for was that scandal shouldn't undermine his Opal authority. His faith in himself was such that until disloyalty was proved to his satisfaction, he would refuse to believe it existed. That was a stand she reluctantly admired, but she resented the manner of his warning to her. True, she would have been more humiliated by his summoning her to his office, but having invited her to dine with him, he could surely have asked her co-operation as an equal? Instead he had accused her of slandermongering and issued his orders to her as 'an employee of Opal'. She didn't want to think about the satisfaction it must have given him to remind her of that!

As if he divined her thoughts Grant said, 'Are you regretting having put yourself in the position of having to take dictation from me?'

'Are you hoping you've made me regret it?' she countered.

He shrugged. 'No feelings either way.'

'But you *had*—strong ones,' she reminded him.

He stood up, forestalling the waiter's reaching for her cape. He put it over her shoulders himself, standing behind her, his hands lingering for a moment. 'Having underrated your stubborn will to show me what a working girl can do,' he remarked as they moved away.

She came back at him quickly. 'And you approve of working girls, don't you?'

'In general, yes.'

'And of Rose de Mille in particular?'

He laughed shortly. 'What a memory! And what a capacity for jealousy! Anyone would suppose you to be a deceived wife——! But yes indeed, I approve of Rose, and for more reasons than that she's a demon for work. Does that answer your question?'

Fern said tartly, 'It wasn't a question. It was a

statement. You make it all too obvious what you think of her, how often and how much.'

'And I daresay you've been kept well posted on that too,' he retorted.

She let that go without comment. Grant drove back to the camp by a different road, passing the creche and the residential bungalows on the way to the main quay. There he parked the car, facing seaward, and sitting forward, arms crossed on the steering-wheel, nodded ahead.

'The object of the evening's exercise,' he said. 'What do you think of it?'

Fern had followed his nod towards the great lighted shape which stood offshore by about half a mile; a ship riding at anchor and yet no ship. She didn't understand him. He had let her suppose he had brought her out in order to issue his warning, and she had begun, 'I thought you——' when he went on, 'The first night shift on the platform. As it's something we have to be proud of, I thought you might like to see it in action. Fine sight, isn't it?'

She was touched by the note of pride in his voice. He had directed a marvel of modern engineering into useful being; not his first nor likely to be his last, but an achievement he needed to show off and be praised for; the eternal male, conscious of his worth but still small-boy vulnerable to opinions he valued. ('Mother, look at the crane I've built; my model of a helter-skelter tower; the elephant I've coloured.') This was Grant, skilled, dominant, arrogant, but wanting her appreciation. *Hers*. If he were truthful, not Rose de Mille's, but hers. She glowed inwardly as she said, meaning it,

'It's magnificent. Have you got a full comple-
ment of men aboard?'

'On continuous shift, and all working like
beavers, quiet as it looks from here.' Still staring
at the rig, he added musingly, almost to himself,
'Odd, the number of chances one is given to set in
motion gear like this that's going to be churning
merrily away, making work and making money,
long after one has moved on oneself. Solemn
thought, that—a kind of immortality while they
last. Brunel with his bridges, Eiffel with his
Tower——' As his voice trailed away into silence
something shame-making, revealing, but wonderful happened to Fern.

If she had had her way with him, she would
have cheated him of even this chance to make and
move on, if he must. As he had accused her, she
would have had him behind a London desk, depriving him of all the future chances before him.
But—and this was the wonderful bit—she had
seen in time the wrong she had done him. Was
seeing it now—from the passenger seat of an open
car, staring at a beaver-busy oil platform, she gave
in unconditionally and had to tell him so.

In future he should go where he liked, and she
would go with him—wherever his job called him.
How had she dared to dictate to him a price for
the loyalty she owed him as his wife? She took it
all back. What he wanted, she wanted for him.
When he was old (she couldn't imagine Grant
old!) he should be able to stab his finger at a globe
and say, 'I laid down oil installations there . . .
and there . . . and there——' All this she had to

say, however incoherently it came out. In a great surge of love which pulsed through her, she laid a hand urgently upon his arm.

'Grant, I——'

At that moment every light on the offshore platform went out.

CHAPTER SIX

GRANT jerked roughly free of her hand. Craning towards the inky darkness, 'What the——? What in the name of fortune's going on?' he muttered.

Bewilderedly Fern looked from him out to sea. 'What's happened? Aren't they supposed to switch off?' she asked foolishly.

He turned on her irritably. 'Be your age, do! It's *a working eight-hour shift*, I told you. No reason to black out *at all*,' he emphasised.

'Then something's wrong?'

'Dynamos cut out, probably. But why?' He stared for a few more minutes, then switched on his engine. 'Look, I've got to wake up the engineers and phone out to the rig. I'll see you back first.'

'Don't bother. It's not on your way. I can walk,' she claimed.

'You'll not walk. Sit tight and hold on, because I'm going to speed,' he warned sharply.

At the creche he leaned to open her door for her but did not get out. Fern scrambled out quickly. 'Let me know what did happen,' she begged. But in slamming the door he might not have heard her, and by the next morning the news was everywhere—the power on the rig had been deliberately sabotaged.

The damage was minor and was rectified within twenty-four hours, but the warning was signifi-

cant, and Fern wondered wryly whether her
scolding by Grant would have been quite as severe
had it happened a day or so earlier. He did not
get in touch with her at all, and she was left to
curse the bitter irony of its having happened just
when it had. Given a few minutes more, even a
moment or two, and she would have blurted out
her surrender. When she had turned to Grant she
hadn't thought what she was going to say. She
had only known that she had to make him understand that on her side their stubborn feud was
over; that she loved him as she always had; that
she was hungry for the forgiveness of his heart,
craved the worship of his body which would tell
her she had it.

Perhaps she wouldn't have needed any words.
Perhaps her seeking of his arms, his lips, would
have said enough to convince him of her sincerity
... But on the heels of that thought came the
chilling memory of the night in Grant's apartment
when he had accused her of tempting him to make
love to her. Supposing, last night, he had made
the same mistake and rejected her again? If so,
the power failure on the rig had saved her, not
betrayed her, and as the days passed with no sign
from Grant, the fire of her courage cooled. If his
wanting her to see the rig in action had been anything more than the showing-off she had judged
it to be; if their evening had ended more abruptly
than he intended, then he knew where she was; at
the end of a telephone line. Without knowing his
mood, she dared not seek another moment of
truth with him, and presently, daunted by his
silence, she hardly regretted the one which had

been snatched from her.

Their next encounter was unplanned on both sides.

Ben was late for an appointment to meet Fern at the Meurice, and she was still waiting for him in the foyer when she saw Grant stroll through from the main bar, to stand, scanning the foyer for a minute or two before, apparently having seen her, he came over.

He stood at her tiny table, a hand on its second chair. 'Am I intruding?' he asked.

'For the moment, no,' she said coolly.

'Then may I?' He sat down. 'What are you drinking?'

'Nothing. I'm waiting for Ben. We had a date for him to take me to the Casino, but he hasn't arrived yet.'

Grant's eyes glinted mockingly. 'He's stood you up? Shame on the man!'

'It needn't be his fault. He never knows when he may be called out on a case. He's sure to ring me before long if he can't make it,' she claimed.

'Tch, tch!' Grant pretended concern. 'The hazards of a medic's girl-friend—too bad. However, who am I to talk? I'm in much the same case myself. Rose, my own date, seems to have let me down, so perhaps you and I should console each other? Drown our sorrows, as they say, in our cups?'

'Rose de Mille? Isn't she singing tonight?' Fern asked.

'Sunday,' Grant reminded her. 'The management gives her every other one off, and there are no rules against followers.'

'So you "follow"?' Fern's tone was dry.

'Sometimes I have to stand in line.' He signalled a waiter. 'Look, we may have to wait some time, and you can't let me drink alone. Just an innocuous tomato juice or a soda?'

She was irritated by his indulgent patronage of her. 'I'd like a brandy,' she told him defiantly, not tempted at all to broach any serious subject to his present facetious mood, but only to keep it at arm's length until Ben came to her rescue.

She saw Grant's eyebrows lift at her order. He knew she didn't like brandy. But he gave it and his own to the waiter, then clasped his hands on the table-top, twiddling his thumbs.

'What shall we talk about?' he enquired. 'Shall we prepare you for the Casino by having a bet on which of our absentee partners shows up first? Or shall we play hide-and-seek ourselves and go dancing somewhere else?'

Fern sipped her brandy, controlling the grimace of distaste for which she guessed he was watching. 'I'm giving Ben another quarter of an hour, and I'm staying here,' she said.

'And then?'

'I shall leave a message at the desk for Ben, and go home.'

'What a wasted evening! Of course I could do the same for Rose, and then you and I could team up as each other's stand-in, why not?'

He was simply making fun of her, and she resented it. 'I don't think that would be a very good idea,' she said.

'Wouldn't it fill a vacuum for both of us?'

'Perhaps. But I'm pretty sure this isn't Ben's fault. And besides——'

But she was thwarted from adding that she had neither the wish nor intention to play proxy for Rose de Mille when, glancing across at the elevators, she saw Rose herself emerge from one of them and start across the foyer. Fern stood up and changed to, 'Besides, the question doesn't arise,' just as Rose reached the table to throw her a cold glance and to confront Grant, now also standing.

'Well, well, to coin a phrase, Better late than——' he began, only to be interrupted by Rose's tart,

'Grant, where have you been? I have waited for you—oh, this half-hour and more. Why have you not kept to our time? What are you doing here?'

He made to take her hand, but she snatched it away. 'Waiting for you,' he told her. 'To the very dot of the time we arranged.'

'But not here!' Rose protested. '*As* we arranged, in your apartment, of course.' After a second of pause she added with telling emphasis for Fern, 'As usual, *mon ami.*'

Grant's quick look was for Fern, who thought, *He realises what Rose has just told me*. But he appeased Rose lightly with, 'Ah then, totally my fault. I should have made the rendezvous more definite when we agreed on "Here". We were up there when we made the date, weren't we? So naturally you understood——' and Fern saw Rose's expression clear into a smug satisfaction before she herself picked up her bag and began to edge round the table.

Grant said, 'Leaving already?'

'Yes. Goodnight.' Her nod included Rose.

He glanced at his watch. 'You're cheating Ben of seven and a half minutes,' he said.

She ignored him and fled to the reception desk, where she was told they had just been about to page her with a message from Ben that an emergency call had prevented his keeping their date. A few minutes earlier she could have been spared the humiliation of Rose's claim that she had been expecting Grant in his penthouse apartment, she thought bitterly. It didn't matter to Fern about who was right about the arrangement; what did matter was Rose's use of the word 'in', rather than 'at'. Mistakenly or not, Rose had been waiting for Grant to go to her there, and that meant she had been accorded the intimacy of a key of her own. Not to be wondered at, Fern supposed, but the brutal fact had been a shock. Rose had been free to let herself in—for what purpose, at nine o'clock at night?

A cosy tête-à-tête dinner ordered from room-service? And after it? Fern's jealous imagination had no difficulty in picturing that aftermath, nor Rose's clandestine return to her own suite in the small hours—even if she left then . . .

The whole episode left a sour taste. If anything were needed to harden Fern's resolve against the surrender to Grant which she had so nearly made, this was it. Now she had proof of how far she had already lost him to Rose de Mille. That evening of the rig failure she could have courted him in vain and already have been too late.

By contrast her work was sanely unemotional, and

by that fact, a kind of balm for her spirit.

The children's world was so down-to-earth, so uncomplicated, their needs so basic, their smiles as ready as their tears, and both evoked and spent for such simple reasons. Rhoda herself was a rock of reassurance that all was right with her small kingdom. She ruled it with a blunt justice which Fern admired greatly, aware as she was that Rhoda's brusquerie was no more than a stout cover for her deep love of all her charges, including their mothers, with whom, on occasion, she could be particularly sharp.

She and Fern were both invited to witness Mahe's marriage ceremony of the anointing of the hands of the bride and groom and the blessing of their house.

'Do we go?' Fern asked.

'Of course. We should give offence if we didn't,' said Rhoda.

'And give presents?'

'If you like. It's not obligatory. It's more important that, having been invited, we be there.'

Fern chose a Maraccan-made bangle of filigree silver for Mahe, and Rhoda, a set of copper cooking-pots. They took a taxi out to Mahe's village on the afternoon of her marriage-day and, along with her family and friends, duly 'witnessed' the simple ceremony by themselves being invited to anoint the couple's hands. Afterwards there was a procession to their new home, a two-roomed cottage thatched with dried palm and banana fronds, where there was a reception on the surrounding patch of parched grass, which seemed to be a free-for-all for the whole village.

Mahe and her Selim made a handsome pair. He earned good money on the tea plantations, he told Fern. He thought Mahe's family were proud to have him as a son-in-law. Buddha would bless him and Mahe with many sons, who would help him on the plantation he would own one day. Yes—in answer to Fern's question as to his family—he had good parents, stern but just, and a clever sister, Vitora, who worked for Opal Oil in the offices, and who was as lovely as she was clever, though lately she seemed a little sad and, loving brother as he was to her, would not tell him why.

Certainly there was no false modesty about Selim Sulong, but he had not exaggerated his sister's looks. Gracefully barefoot in a scarlet sarong, she was tall for a Malay, with a deep rose blush to her skin, an expressive mouth and 'speaking' eyes as black as her luxuriant fall of hair. Produced proudly by Selim, she had a grave sweet smile for Fern and Rhoda, who said at once, 'But I know you, don't I? You work for Opal Oil?'

The girl nodded. 'In the office of Sahib Logan. I open the letters. I speak to the telephone. I make the coffee.'

Fern said, 'Your brother is very happy with Mahe. You are not married yourself?' Perhaps Fern was watching for the sadness of which Selim had spoken, but certainly there was a reserve in Vitora's 'No, I have no husband,' which discouraged further questioning and which Rhoda claimed later she had read as possible jealousy of Selim and Mahe.

'She must be five years older than Mahe, and

she may feel she's on the shelf,' was Rhoda's verdict.

'With those looks?' Fern differed. 'Her village
boys and the men she meets at Opal can't be using
their eyes!'

But Rhoda held to her opinion. 'She must know
she's beautiful and can't understand why nobody
has chosen her yet.'

'She only said she hadn't a *husband*,' Fern
pointed out.

'Though without adding a claim to going steady
with a boy-friend, which most girls would in self-
defence if they had one. Well, wouldn't *you*?'
Rhoda retorted—unanswerably by Fern who, in
Grant and Ben, could be said to have both—and
neither.

Her relationship with Ben was a constant worry
to her. He assumed so certainly that, off duty from
the creche, they would always be at each other's
disposal, that any evenings she spent alone or with
Rhoda became rare interruptions to those he
begged her to spend with him. She liked him, was
grateful for their companionship, and admired
him for the ambition of which he talked a lot. His
courting of her was ardent but controlled, because, he confessed, he had ideals about wanting
his wife to be virgin when they married, leaving
her in little doubt that she was the girl he hoped
would travel at his side when he 'moved on'—an
impossibility she could not bring herself to break
to him, though she knew she ought.

She couldn't tell him why, and he wouldn't
understand. Increasingly she dreaded the day of
reckoning which would part them, but supposed

it wasn't upon her yet. Until suddenly it was.

It began with Ben's being called to Grant's office at the end of his children's clinic at the creche, and when he came back Rhoda had already gone to her lunch in the canteen, and Fern was still clearing up after the morning's work. She sensed his excitement at once. 'Great news!' he announced, catching her by the waist and waltzing her round. 'What do you think? Guess!'

Fern pulled free of him and quipped lightly, 'Your invention for the cure of the common cold has proved a world-beater, and you've been awarded a putty medal for your research.'

Ben grinned. 'I should be so lucky! But no, seriously—Headquarters are engaging staff for the new project in Brazil!'

'And——?' Fern prompted.

'*And,*' he emphasised, 'the plant needs a Medical Officer, *and* Boss Wilder has recommended me!'

For a reason he couldn't know, Fern's heart sank. 'Oh, Ben,' she breathed faintly, 'if the job is offered to you, will you accept? Does it mean promotion?'

'Moneywise, some,' he bubbled. 'But it's the move, on Grant's backing, that's the importance for me. And knowing pretty surely that I'd jump at the chance, he'd promised me to them before he bearded me.'

'And so you'll be going?'

'If I'd had any doubts, Grant would have refused to listen. For the sake of my future he's practically ordered me out, and I'm as good as on my way.' Ben added softly, 'On *our* way, Fern?' putting a question.

But Fern, chilled to her core, had a question of her own. 'Did Grant Wilder tell you specifically he was letting you go for your own good?'

'More or less in those very words, and I believe him. He's the best of guys.' Ben paused. 'But you heard me, darling? I said "on *our* way", and you understood?'

She was appalled by a view of Grant's duplicity which she must not betray to Ben, who thought Grant 'the best of guys'. She said hesitantly, 'Yes, I think I understood, and I'm very, very grateful. But it's impossible, you know. You'll go to Brazil, and I'm more than glad for you. But you'll go from here alone. I shan't be with you.'

Ben frowned, working that out. 'You mean you can't leave Rhoda flat without an assistant? Well, that's all right. I have to work out a month's notice myself. More than enough time for Rhoda to look around, and for you to get ready to marry me here before we go. Or we could do it in England. You'll want to go back, I daresay——' He broke off, as if expecting her eager agreement, and when it did not come, he reached for both her hands and held on as he added, 'It's nothing more serious, is it? I know I haven't proposed before now. But was it necessary? Haven't we both known for a long time—about us?' His face clouded. 'At least *I've* known. Haven't you?'

Fern shook her head. 'No, Ben,' she said.

'*No?*'

'No.' As he drew breath for another protest, she said again, 'No, but I've been terribly wrong about that.' Avoiding his hurt, accusing eyes, she stared down at their linked hands. 'I've been so happy with our friendship and our being together, but you've always been frank about your needing to move on . . . and on, until you reached whatever full stop you planned would content you. And as I've always known I'm not the girl who could move on with you, I haven't let myself get too fond of you, and I hoped you weren't too serious about me.'

'You must have known I love you,' he reproached her. 'As for the itching feet business, there's no reason why we couldn't come to terms on that. Only needs a bit of give and take——'

She shook her head again. 'No. There's no reason in the world why you should curb yourself for me when—I wish I hadn't to say this, my dear—when I don't love you enough.'

He winced as if she had struck him. 'Hm, straight from the shoulder. But if I love *you* enough, and I wouldn't expect too much of you, wouldn't that do?'

'Ben, you know it wouldn't,' she argued. 'You deserve a girl who'll go willingly with you wherever you go, and I'm not that girl. And there's something else. You set too high a standard for me. You've always said you wanted to be the first man for the girl you marry. And—well, you wouldn't be that for me. I've been in love before.'

She was praying he wouldn't make her put the full meaning of that into words, and he did not. But he dropped her hands and after a moment or two there was an edge of bitterness to his question, 'And what happened?'

'We—parted.'

'Why?'

She told the truth. 'For the same reason that would come between you and me. I didn't *want* a marriage that would have to be kept going on a kind of gipsy trail about the earth. I wanted a home and——'

'And when you told your bloke so, you split?' Ben cut in.

'Yes.'

'But you're still in love with him?'

'For my sins, yes. I realise I was mad and wrong, but it's too late now.'

'Needn't be, if he hasn't married somebody else,' said Ben. But understandably his next thought was for himself, rather than for her, when he went on, 'I never guessed. You've seemed so open and free and—sort of untouched. But if you're still in love with him, that does wrap things up between you and me, doesn't it? I've loved you and wanted you, Fern, but not with your head turned back over your shoulder at another man, and not if you couldn't share my life as I mean it to go.' He turned aside, his mouth working. 'Don't worry for me, will you? I'm grateful for everything I've had from you, and you can't say we haven't had fun?'

Near to tears herself, 'Yes, we've had fun, and thank you for all of it,' Fern agreed, watching him to the door where he paused and looked back.

'Perhaps Grant would waive my month's notice here and let me go at once. Since it's curtains for us, mightn't that be best?' he appealed.

'Oh, Ben——' She gestured emptily without

replying. She hadn't the right to choose the time of their parting, and if Grant's motives were as she suspected, he probably meant Ben's month of notice to be a piece of refined torture for her by depriving her piecemeal of Ben's friendship, instead of in one decisive cut. He could be relishing the image of their having to work side by side with the prospect of the coming break hanging over them . . . At the thought she wondered sickly how much more erosion could her love take from his humiliations of her before it turned to hate.

In answer to Ben's question she told him, 'I'd rather it were that way, yes.'

He nodded agreement. 'So would I. You can't want to see me around, and I can't bear to be. I'll go and see Grant again in the morning.'

'He may not want to listen,' Fern warned. But the door had already closed upon Ben, leaving her resolved upon one thing.

She had to see Grant before Ben did. She had to learn the truth of this latest move against her, and only Grant could tell her that.

CHAPTER SEVEN

SHE looked at her watch—it was seven o'clock—and laid her plans.

Ben wouldn't seek Grant out tonight. But she must. He wouldn't be in his office until now, and if he were at the Club she couldn't beard him there. But she had to find out, so without giving her name she rang Le Corsair, to hear from a friendly porter that Grant was not in his room, nor on the Club premises. He often drove into the city at about this time, the man volunteered. Perhaps the Mem could try his apartment at the Meurice?

The Mem could—but she wasn't going to give him prior notice of her urgency by telephone. She must go herself. If Grant weren't there she wouldn't know where next to look for him. But if he were, they couldn't have a more private place for her purpose. Always supposing he was alone there, she thought cynically, which he might well not be.

She rang for a taxi to come out for her and left a message for Rhoda to say she had gone into town.

At the Meurice she strolled round the crowded foyer, looked into the bars and the dining-room, hoping Grant wouldn't be there.

He wasn't, and she took the elevator to the penthouse floor. Her knock at his door was answered by Grant in a short towelling robe, his thumb marking his place in the book in his hand. At sight of Fern his eyes narrowed in an ironic smile. 'Well, well,' he drawled, 'I should have laid money on how long it would take you to contact me, shouldn't I?'

That she hadn't surprised him disconcerted her. She had rehearsed her indignation and it was galling to find it was expected of her. She said, 'You knew then that I should see through your scheme to get rid of one of my two real friends on the island, and that I should lose no time in telling you so?'

He stood aside for her to go in, and closed the door behind her. 'More or less,' he agreed. 'Counting on your ability to pre-judge any motives of mine, I thought you couldn't fail to bang the drum on Ben's behalf, with or without his consent.'

'Well, someone had to,' she retorted. '*He* sees you as his fairy godfather, granting him an opportunity he's been hoping for. He doesn't know, as I suspected at once, that you cut it to measure for him, simply to punish me!'

Grant studied her for a long moment. 'You think you know that, and you mean Ben to know it too?' he asked.

She shook her head. 'No. I wouldn't disillusion him about you. He'll go to Brazil, believing you're a great guy and never guessing that you'd stoop to anything so petty as getting rid of him in order to part him from me.'

'H'm—pretty crafty of me to have created a job for Ben in Brazil, where I have no influence at all,' was Grant's dry comment on that.

Fern's gesture was impatient. 'I'm only saying you saw the advantage to yourself in offering it to Ben and seeing that he took it.'

'He didn't need much persuading.'

'Of course not. You knew you could count on his ambition to move on. That's why your making use of it's so despicable. You've hated our going about together, and this was your way of putting an end to it. Well, you've succeeded, and I hope you're satisfied!'

Grant said, 'That's just nursery defiance. You needed to get this off your chest, but you don't hope I'm satisfied. You'd like me to be wallowing in remorse.'

'I doubt if you've enough conscience,' she flung at him.

'For having put Ben Croftus in the way of his dearest wish?'

'For doing it for the mean reason you did.'

'And if I agree my motives were questionable, it doesn't occur to you that they were wholly concerned to effect a rescue mission for Ben?' Grant paused. 'Rescue from you, my dear, no less.'

Fern gasped. '*Rescue?* He didn't need rescuing! He—he's in love with me!'

'Exactly. Heading for danger at the gallop, if he isn't already up to his neck.' Both hands in the pockets of his robe, Grant strolled towards her. Closer, as he stood above her, she was headily aware of his body's familiar, personal scent and, for all her recoil from his malice, found herself longing to touch ... and be touched. Looking down at her, he went on, 'Because you're a danger to a man—you were to me, you are to Ben. Your looks, those green pools you call eyes, your body, that—charisma, that appeal——' He broke off. 'At a guess, Ben is far enough gone to ask you to go with him to Brazil, and you've refused?'

'Yes.'

'Of course. No blind "Whither thou goest, I will go", no cap over the windmill for you, no world well lost. There wasn't for me and there wouldn't be for Ben. You were right when you said once I should warn him about your affair, not you. Something along the lines of *La Belle Dame Sans Merci*—"You've got yourself a lovely lady without pity there, mate. Too bad." But if he's going to Brazil without you, perhaps he's seen the red light for himself before it's too late,' Grant concluded.

She had achieved nothing and had collected only his scorn by her errand. She said flatly, 'Ben is going to ask you to let him go at once, without working out his notice.'

'Just as well. He can be off as soon as I can get a replacement.' Over his shoulder as Grant turned away and began a leisurely discarding of his robe, he asked, 'How did you come tonight?'

'By taxi.'

'And you've kept it waiting?'

'Yes,' she lied. She hadn't.

'Good. Because I'm sorry, I'm between showering and changing and keeping a date.' He shrugged back into the sleeves of the robe and crossed to open the door for her. Fern went out, dismissed.

A few days later Ben's successor flew in from South Africa, and Ben was free to leave as soon as he had briefed Dr Verhout, a middle-aged Dutchman, on the job. Meanwhile, though Fern would have liked to know what had passed between Ben and Grant when his month's notice had been waived, Ben had simply reported that Grant had been agreeable, and since then had either avoided her or was professionally cool when they met.

She had no right to be hurt. He could have embarrassed her much more if he hadn't taken her refusal as final. But she was going to miss him, and she mentally writhed at the thought of the satisfaction it must have given Grant to break up a friendship which had been so lightheartedly blameless, even on Ben's side.

Dangerous, he had called her! For being herself. For being humanly responsive and outgoing in gratitude for being liked and sought-after and her companionship enjoyed. Wasn't she still the girl he had courted and loved with passion until their wills had clashed? He hadn't thought of her as dangerous then. Why had he to scourge her with the accusation now—now that it no longer mattered to him what she was or did or became?

There was a party at the Club for Ben's last night in Maracca. It was strictly stag, for which Fern was thankful, as Grant was sure to be there. She was dreading a private parting from Ben, but he didn't ask this of her. Considerate of her to the last, he shared his goodbyes between her and Rhoda and the children at the creche. He had gifts for all of them, and the occasion became a party, with everyone getting hugged and kissed all round, and Ben being waved away in a clamour of good wishes in which his pressure of Fern's hand and his whispered, 'Not your fault. Bless you for everything,' went unnoticed.

It was typical of Rhoda's reserve that she had accepted Ben's and Fern's growing intimacy with only a tacit approval, and to Fern's relief her acceptance of Ben's abrupt departure was equally incurious. She chose to regard it as a strictly professional move without any personal strings, and her only sign of being aware that it had broken up anything for them was her cryptic compliment to Fern, 'Bad enough losing Ben, without losing you too,' which showed she knew there were questions which might be asked, but which she saw as none of her business.

It was an attitude which Fern had to wish more people took. For the most part, their comments on her lack of dates with Ben for evenings on the town or tennis or swimming were not unkind, and there were plenty of candidates for filling the vacuum for her. But in the narrow community of the camp there was also the gossip, perhaps not meant for her ears, but which reached them nevertheless.

She had ditched Ben because, as Sir Manfred's daughter, she considered he wasn't a good enough prospect. He had ditched her because he had heard she was playing around with someone else.

Grant Wilder hadn't initially offered the Brazil
job to Ben; it was Ben, disillusioned and wretched,
who had asked for his cards and got them, just
when the job happened to be going . . . And the
proof of all this? Well, Fern and Ben hadn't been
seen together from the very day Ben announced
his departure, had they?

So the idle stories went, and Fern had to learn
to ignore them. She understood that curiosity
needed to embroider them, but she was at a complete loss over the theory that she had double-
crossed Ben with another man, until by evil
chance she found herself captive to Freda Logan
again.

They both went to the same hairdresser in the
city, and were together in the salon's waiting room
while awaiting their appointments. When Fern
was shown in by the receptionist, Freda abandoned her glossy magazine and allowed herself a
thin smile of welcome.

'You're quite a stranger to town these days,'
she told Fern. 'We used to see so much of you
before Ben Croftus left. In fact, I've heard it
wondered that either of you ever managed to do
any work. But that was just malicious talk, of
course. You know what people are!'

Fern said with fervent candour, 'I do indeed.'

'Yes, well, you two were so close that we were
all expecting wedding bells, when suddenly Ben's
off like a scalded cat, and no one knows what his
haste could have been.'

'Really?' Fern picked up a magazine and riffled
through its pages. 'That's odd. From the various
versions I've heard, I thought quite a lot of people

claimed to know why he left as suddenly as he did.'

Freda looked as if she had been cheated out of a scoop. 'Oh, you know then what's being said?' she asked flatly.

'Wasn't I meant to?' Fern countered. 'After all, if I didn't know Ben's reasons were being discussed, how could I be expected to tell you all which theory was right and which was wrong?'

Missing the irony in Fern's tone, Freda sat forward eagerly. 'Then there *was* something personal about his going as he did? Something involving you?' she almost begged.

Fern said, 'Well, naturally, considering the friends Ben and I were. I think I was the first person he told that he'd been offered and was taking this job in Brazil.'

'Just—told you? No more than that?' Freda laughed off the disappointment in her voice by adding, 'Really, rumour does run riot, given its head! Do you realise you're supposed to have jilted Ben out of hand, told him you'd only been playing him along for amusement? My dear, a whole gaggle of our friends believe that!'

'So I understand,' said Fern.

Freda hurried on, 'And a lot more who think that if there was jilting, it was on Ben's side, because he'd found you were carrying on with Grant Wilder behind his back——' At the sound of Fern's sharply caught breath of shock, she checked, then went on, 'Yes, I know; too absurd, you may think, to give Ben or anyone the chance to suspect you of raising any action there. But I'm afraid I do have to confess that *I* may be a little to blame over that, when I was indiscreet enough to tell someone that I knew you'd gone up to his apartment one evening—alone. Naughty of me not to hold my tongue, perhaps. But we all know the de Mille visits him there, so why not you too? At a different time, of course, understood!'

Remembering her search through the foyer and bars of the Meurice in search of Grant, Fern said, 'I don't recall seeing you on the one night I did go up to Grant Wilder's apartment by myself. So how do you know I went?'

'I'd been to the powder-room and I was leaving the other elevator when I heard you tell the page, "the penthouse floor", and I was with some people having a drink in the foyer when you came down again.'

'Very soon after I'd gone up, I think?' Fern invited.

'Oh, quite,' Freda agreed amiably. 'Of course you couldn't have been—well, *up* to anything in that time, could you? And that's where I was so wrong. Instead of passing on what I'd seen when people began to talk, I should have kept it to myself and warned you instead about playing with fire in that quarter. Tempting, of course, if you're attracted, but the man is dynamite to women—dynamite, no less!'

Despising herself for discussing Grant, Fern couldn't help suggesting, 'I thought he was supposed to be fully occupied with Rose de Mille?'

Freda echoed, 'Fully? My dear, a man of Grant Wilder's appetites is rarely fully taken up with one woman. You should hear of his reputation in his office! He's such a satyr with the girls there that none of them ever feels safe. Which is why you really shouldn't demean yourself by——' She broke off as her stylist appeared in the doorway. 'Ah, Toya, you're ready for me now?' but before she left with the girl she added to Fern, 'If our friend isn't very careful, he could find himself in a very sticky situation one of these days—you'll see!'

So that was how the story of Ben's jilting of herself had started, thought Fern, convinced that no one would have linked her with Grant since the early days of his escorting her, unless Freda Logan had produced that evidence of her visit to his flat. She had little doubt that Freda's fiction had made it into a prolonged assignation; even hinted that it was a regular happening to which Ben, learning of it, had reacted with jealous finality.

But angry as she was, Fern felt powerless. She had no proof but her intuition's conviction that Freda had ever reported anything more sensational than the truth of her visit to Grant. Freda could deny—her word against Fern's—that she had ever made scandal of it. As for those hints about Grant's promiscuity, Fern knew she must not let them upset her unduly. Freda could well have made them up on the spot, and thrown in her parting threat for good measure. Grant's confident egoism was too much its own man to need bolstering with a series of undercover affairs with his own staff. She hadn't to be afraid for him there . . .

Now that Ben had gone she was infinitely lonely, longing for someone in whom she could confide. But how could she, even in Rhoda, who had taken her on trust as had everyone else? It was too late now to lay public claim to that wedding ring in Grant's bureau drawer. If she did, Grant would never forgive her for putting him in the same false position as she would be in herself, and the only way out for her, if not for him, would be the empty surrender of giving up her job at the creche and going home, leaving behind an impossible situation for him. No, she couldn't do that to him. When she went home to England, as she foresaw she must very soon, she would have to go as the Fern Stirling everyone in Maracca believed her to be.

In her letters to Sir Manfred she took a scrupulous pride in writing as cheerfully as possible and, in obedience to Grant's ruling, quoting no gossip of which he could disapprove.

Not that the current wave of the camp's internal troubles could be dismissed as mere gossip any longer. They were facts. It was no secret that, since the sabotage on the rig, Grant had to deal almost daily with the impact of major or minor spanners in the works.

Derricks broke down. Parcels of tools went missing. There was an abortive attempt at arson. Austin Logan was obstructive to a point of dumb insolence, and in her own mind Fern was sure Grant must know that much of the trouble was Logan-inspired if not actually executed. But whether or not he had reported to Headquarters on his second-in-command, Grant had made no open move against him, when he himself was caught by events for which the evidence came from quite another quarter than either Austin or Freda Logan.

Without being aware of the import of Vitora Sulong's absence, Fern missed the girl from the office one day when she went to get some supply requisitions for the creche countersigned by Austin. Since they had met at Mahe's wedding and Fern had learned where Vitora worked, they had always exchanged smiles and a few words when they met. Today, on her way out of the office, Fern asked where Vitora was.

'She is not here,' said the girl Fern had stopped.

'No. She's away just for today? She's not ill?' Fern asked.

Vitora's workmate showed white teeth in an embarrassed smile. 'No, she is not ill, Vitora. Just—not here. Not yesterday, not today, not any day soon, I think,' she said, making a mystery of Vitora's absence which Fern realised she didn't mean to solve.

Back at the creche Fern's mention of the incident evoked no surprise from Rhoda, who replied in her usual shorthand, 'Yes. Been given leave of absence. Three months pregnant.'

'Oh dear! She told us at Mahe's wedding that she wasn't married,' Fern said with a shocked sigh. 'How do you know?'

'Doc Verhout was called to her. She fainted in the office, and was sent home. Wouldn't name the father then, but she's told him since.'

'Who? A boy from her village? Or someone on the camp?'

Rhoda shrugged. 'Professional etiquette. Doc wouldn't have told me if I'd asked. I wasn't risking that snub.'

'Of course you couldn't,' Fern agreed, neither of them knowing then that someone other than the doctor had broached the girl's confidence, for a day or two later it was common knowledge that she had claimed Grant to be the father.

The effect upon a community which thrived on personal news was sensational. For Fern it was almost totally shattering. Never, until that last meeting with Freda Logan, had she heard Grant accused of womanising among his staff, and so sure had she been that he wouldn't stoop to it that she had discounted Freda's hints as mere jealous ravings on Freda's part.

But this news had come from Vitora Sulong herself, in the first place to her doctor and then, possibly, to her family, who had made no secret of it. Fern, remembering Vitora's brother's claim that their parents were 'stern but just', wondered whether they had had to wrest Grant's name from the girl and what their intentions were, now they had it. Fern also wondered about Rose de Mille's reaction to the story when it reached her. Would she, after a first recoil of jealousy and disbelief, want to rally to Grant's defence against all the calumny about to pour upon his head? If Rose loved Grant, she would. For, after the initial shock, that was Fern's own fighting response to the situation—a dilemma in which Grant could rarely have found himself;

publicly in the wrong, his back to the wall, facing, if nothing worse, all the blame and snide comments and ostracism his world could deal out to him.

Through all that Fern, loving him, wanted to range herself on his side; longed for him to know she was there and to need her there. But how, in the cold climate of his scorn and indifference, was she to convey that to him? Supposing she had another chance like the one the crisis on the rig had foiled—supposing she could tell him that nothing between them, nothing between him and Rose, nothing between him and Vitora Sulong, could kill her enduring love, would he listen, understand, forgive? Lest he shouldn't believe her, she was afraid to try.

Far from appearing to have his back to any wall, Grant rode the affair with aloof disdain for the rising tide of criticism about it and his leadership in general. He asked advice of no one, admitted nothing, denied nothing. Vitora did not return to the office. She stayed at home where, rumour had it, she was receiving regular payments from Grant.

This was confirmed by Mahe on a visit to Rhoda and Fern, and to spend a morning with 'her' children.

'Vitora has money sent to her every week in the mail,' Mahe said. 'Selim does not know how much, but it is more than she was paid in the Opal office. Selim is sad for her. He hoped, as she is so clever, that she would become a real secretary and work a typewriter. But he thinks Sahib Grant has told her she must not work while she awaits the baby, and she obeys him.'

'Sees the doctor for your district, does she?' asked Rhoda.

'When he comes to the village, yes. But she is well,' said Mahe.

'And her parents? How do they take it?'

'At first Selim's father was very angry with Vitora. But he listens to Selim, who tells him, what is done, is done, and he and her mother begin to be content that she will give them a grandchild.'

Rhoda was looking at Mahe's figure. 'Which you hope to do too, no doubt?'

Mahe looked downcast. 'For me, not yet. I had hoped that Vitora's little one would not be so far ahead of mine that they could run and play together,' she mourned, though Rhoda consoled, 'At that stage, a year or even two between them won't make much difference.'

Grant's son—toddling and chattering, laughing and crying in surroundings which no one could foresee for him while Grant kept his own counsel and no one dared question him about the affair. Fern was thankful that neither Rhoda nor Mahe could have an inkling of how every word of discussion of it seemed to run a knife through her heart. Before Mahe left that morning, Fern made herself ask whether Grant ever visited Vitora. But Mahe said No, as far as any of them knew, he did not see her. There was just the money in the post. That was all.

For a time Fern wondered if he would see it as his duty to tell her why and how it had all happened, and what were his plans for the girl. But when he gave no sign of considering she had a right to know, she realised how far he must have moved from thinking of her as his wife, and that probably Rose de Mille could demand and get explanations he would not offer to her. How much had he admitted to Sir Manfred—if anything, at this stage? And how was she to write to her father as if there were still nothing sinister to report about either Grant's standing with his team or with his personal affairs?

She had neither written nor telephoned to Perth when the awaited summons to her from Grant came. He phoned from his office, inviting her to dine. The Meurice was rather public, but he would book a table there, unless she preferred somewhere quieter?

For *this* meeting—possibly their last, for their leavetaking of each other after everything necessary had been said between them, certainly she wanted somewhere quieter! 'Your apartment?' she suggested.

'Very well. I'll call for you. Eight o'clock.'

'No.' Rhoda probably wouldn't ask questions, but Fern didn't want to admit to dining with Grant. 'I'll meet you in the residents' lounge of the Meurice,' she said.

When she reached the hotel she was sick with apprehension, dreading the hatching of fresh scandal about Grant if they were seen together. But he was waiting for her at the entrance instead of in the lounge, and took her straight across the foyer to the bank of elevators, where they had one to themselves up to his floor.

The dinner table was laid in his living-room and all the dishes were cold—a vichyssoise soup, a fish mousse and salad, and a pavlova of passion fruit. Fern guessed Grant had ordered the meal in order to dispense with a waiter, and felt a twinge of resentment that he recognised too their need to be clandestine.

He poured the wine, served her with soup and appeared to be prepared to postpone any of the discussion he had summoned her to until after they had eaten. But this was too much for Fern's racked nerves. Fingering the stem of her wine-glass, she said, 'This isn't a social occasion for us, is it? So oughtn't you to tell me straight away what it's about?'

He looked at her over his own glass. 'And spoil what I'd hoped could be a pleasant, undisturbed dinner?' he queried.

That boded ill. 'Need it be spoiled by what you have to say to me?' she asked.

He shrugged. 'Meetings between us usually have the effect of spoiling whatever follows them, I've noticed.'

'Then if you know that, why bother to ask me to dinner at all?' she parried.

He put down his glass, spread his napkin and took up his soup spoon. 'Because,' he said firmly, 'I had, and still have, no intention of letting our dinner be spoiled. So drink up and enjoy the rest of what our good chef has sent you under my orders to make at least the meal a memorable pleasure for us. It's my contribution to the evening. What you choose to make of yours can very well wait to be seen.'

What could he mean? And how could he be so debonair under the clouds of his involvement with three women, not to mention those which the jealousy of enemies had gathered for him? Giving in, Fern did her best with the delicious soup, and as the wine took effect, made a passable effort with the other courses. They kept up an impersonal conversation of sorts, Grant appearing completely untroubled, she trying hard to play the part of his dinner guest with nothing hanging over her, and not succeeding very well.

When at last he offered a selection of liqueurs with her coffee, she absently chose one, but did not touch it or the coffee when he brought them to her chair at the uncurtained window which looked out over the light-studded darkness to the infinite darkness of the open sea.

Not looking at him, she said, 'We can't postpone this any longer. Why had you to see me?'

Grant drew up a chair beside hers. 'To give you some news which I feel is your due.'

'What news? Or can I guess?' she added quickly, in an effort to hold off shock for a moment.

'I shouldn't think so. It isn't public property yet,' he said.

'If it's anything fresh about yourself, it soon will be. You should know that,' Fern pointed out.

He shook his head. 'Not this time, until I choose to make it public. It's come in on a scrambled code from Headquarters. I'm to leave Maracca for a new Opal field off the coast of

Norway, trouble-shooting some of the problems it's going to face next winter.'

Fern gasped. Was he running away, or had he been ordered out on the evidence of his enemies? 'But they made you manager here. I thought it was a permanency,' she protested. 'Who's taking your place? Austin Logan? Wh—when are you to go?'

He ignored her protest, and took her questions in turn. 'Not Logan. He isn't equal to the job. They'll bring in a new management wallah when I go—which is an open date so far, giving me time to wind up my affairs here.'

(Your relationship with Rose de Mille; your obligations to Vitora Sulong. Even if Vitora can be fobbed off with money, I must be an obstacle to your settling with your other woman, thought Fern.) Scorning to taunt him with either of their names, she said, 'And I suppose you had to tell me about this because I'm one of your affairs that need to be wound up?'

'Well, naturally,' he agreed, as if surprised she should ask. 'Did you suppose I should hi-tail out into the wide blue yonder without letting you know I was on my way?'

'Father did just that to me—with your help,' she reminded him bitterly.

'Even so. This is different. We've the same legal claims on each other as we ever had, and at least the moral duty, I'd think, to report on our future movements and plans. And so—*I* am going to Norway. What are you going to do?'

Fern heard his question in dismay and despair. She had half hoped, almost expected, waited for it to be different. Waited to hear him ask, 'Will you come with me this time?'—and he hadn't said it. Instead he had coolly invited her to suggest plans as detached and self-interested as his own.

As she sipped her cooling coffee she asked, 'Does Father know about this?'

'I believe he master-minded the offer to me.'

'Do you want to go?'

'With reservations, yes. To coin a phrase, "It will make a nice change".'

She waited again, then was forced by his silence to comment, 'From Maracca to a Norwegian winter—I should think so!' An imp of malice added, 'I can't say I envy you.'

'I thought you wouldn't.' His conclusive tone told her it was useless to wait any longer for what she wanted to hear, and he went on to press, 'You haven't answered my question—what do you intend to do?'

'I don't know. You've sprung this on me. I like it here. I've made friends. So I daresay'—making it up as she went along—'I shall stay until Father goes back to England, when I shall probably go home too.'

He nodded, as if that sounded reasonable. 'You're a free agent,' he said. He stood when she did and turned with her towards the door. 'Thank you for making me the first to hear about your going,' Fern told him. 'You'll let me know when——?'

They might have been exchanging small talk at the end of a party—two near-strangers about to ~o their separate ways—when Grant said suddenly, 'You know, I begin to think that Sir Manfred had something when he once told me we were our own worst enemies, you and I.'

Fern halted to stare at him. 'What did he mean? In what connection?'

'I don't remember. But in general he was right, of course, and I've often thought since that we'd have been a wiser two people, if not a couple, supposing we'd had ourselves a fiery tempest of an affair, and then have been able to wave each other an airy "Nice to have known you" goodbye.'

She felt sick with disappointment. 'You say you've thought that?' she managed shakily.

'On occasion.' He paused. Then: 'We could still allow ourselves the "nice knowing you" bit, perhaps?' he suggested at the moment in which she knew he was going to take her in his arms and that she wasn't going to resist them.

They went round her, crushing her against him. Her bag, slung over her arm, swung against his thigh. Impatiently he wrenched it free, flung it aside and drew her to him again. His lips found hers, willingly parted to the coaxing invitation of his kiss which turned from a first soft caress to a hot insistence on its right to explore, to tantalise, to arouse.

This was nothing like his savage, uncaring assault to her body on the last night they had shared before they had parted. This was a tentative making-love, purposeful but patient; a willingness to wait for her desire to leap to meet his; the male's courting of the female which was common to all nature and which man brought to a worshipful art in the wooing of his woman.

And Fern surrendered to it, her senses all-yielding, all-responsive, her reason blinded and still. As Grant's hands moved seductively, twisting a strand of her hair into a curling tress, smoothing the curve of her body from the shoulder he had bared to the dip of her waist and the swell of her thigh, she heard herself making soft little croons of delight. Until—unbidden, irrelevant and unwelcome, the word 'expertise' thrust itself into her mind, shrinking and shrivelling her desire for Grant as if it were struck by frost.

Expertise. It was the perfect glove-fit word for—all this. With this gentle appeal and understanding of the need to woo, he would have won Rose de Mille, if not others before her. With the same he would have seduced Vitora Sulong, and now he was using it successfully upon herself—*'No!'* Her denial was a shout and the violence of her recoil from Grant wrenched her from his hold.

They stood, panting like two animals at bay. Then Grant said, 'No?' as a question, and her dumb nod agreed. She drew up the shoulder of her dress and he handed her bag to her.

' "No", with any reason I'd be likely to appreciate?' he enquired.

She shook her head miserably. 'It's all false—now. It's too late.' Too late after Rose; too late after Vitora—he *must* understand!

'I see,' he said. He went with her to the door and through it. But when he made to close it behind them both, Fern said again, 'No,' turning it to a request with, 'Please,' and, 'Let me go home alone.'

He took her to the elevator, put her into it and stood back. 'I'll ring for a taxi for you from here. Collect it at the entrance,' he said, letting her have her way.

CHAPTER EIGHT

THERE were flowers for Fern the next morning, a
sheaf of exotics, scented frangipani, spray orchids
and passion flowers. In Grant's writing the flor-
ist's card read on one side—'While it lasted, it
was . . .' and on the other '. . . nice knowing you',
the cool finality of the words bringing an agonis-
ing ache to her throat in her fight against futile
tears.

Now she remembered how, before last night,
she had seen herself as Grant's ally against his
world, whose love could surmount and forgive
anything, even his faithless pursuit and conquest
of the two other women in his life. Yet last night
she had cravenly waited for an invitation which
had not come, and in his arms she hadn't even
fought the jealous torture of 'These hands moved
just so over their bodies. These lips kissed *them*'.
She had let it ride her into a physical revulsion
which belied every welcoming response she made.
She had failed Grant, and a second chance to
stand by him would not come again.

She gave a lot of thought to her own plans. She
loved working at the creche and felt she had a
duty to Rhoda to stay as long as possible. She had
earned a kind of happiness in Maracca at the price
of losing Grant, but when he had gone she would
have to come to terms with a life without him. As
time went on it should become easier to answer to

her maiden name without the pang of guilt she
had on every occasion that she heard it now, and
while there was no home for her to return to in
England, she might as well stay.

She reached her decision without enthusiasm,
but she wrote as much to her father, telling him
she knew of Grant's projected move to Norway,
but she wouldn't go back to London until after
Sir Manfred's own return there. In her first draft
of her letter she added a rather cynical 'Sorry your
idea in bringing me here hasn't worked out.
However, thank you for the experience all the
same.' But she made a second copy, leaving that
out. That same experience had taught her that 'I
told you so' was a pretty empty triumph at best.

Her days at the creche passed without any more
stirring event than a false measles alarm and a
week's supply of ice cream—the creche's highest
award for virtue—having gone missing from its
unloading at the docks. Until the morning when
Mahe arrived, dishevelled from her long hot walk
from her village and more disturbed in her
Eastern serenity than either Rhoda or Fern had
ever seen her.

'It is trouble for us, for our family!' she panted.
'Vitora has left her home, gone away. Tells no
one, not Selim, not anyone, where she goes . . .
why she goes. Oh, Mem Camell'—Mahe clutched
at both Rhoda's hands—'tell us, please, Mem,
what to do? She leaves no word, no written thing
for her mother and father. But she is gone!'

Calmly Rhoda detached the clinging hands,
said, 'Coffee!' to Fern from the corner of her
mouth and put the distraught girl into a chair.

When Fern brought the coffee Mahe grasped at the mug, and while she gulped thirstily, Rhoda reported the little she had learned.

Vitora had slept at home as usual last night. This morning she had gone, taking a very few possessions with her, but such money as her parents thought she had. Her father had run to his son's cottage with the news. But Selim had left for the sugar plantation at dawn, and Mahe, not knowing how to advise Vitora's father, had come to Mem Camell for help. In the same kind of aside as she had ordered coffee for Mahe, Rhoda muttered to Fern, 'If this is Grant Wilder's doing, I'll have his blood!' Of Mahe she asked gently, 'None of you thought that the father of the baby she is having might have sent for her, or come to take her away, hm?'

Mahe flushed. 'The—father? But he is——'

'Yes,' Rhoda cut in, 'we know. Vitora told you, didn't she, he is Sahib Grant?'

Mahe nodded. 'But he would not—— He sends money for the baby. But he would not——' she fumbled confusedly '—would not want to take her to him as his wife. She is Malay girl and Buddhist. It would not be right.'

'To which there's a coarse retort which I won't make,' said Rhoda, again in aside to Fern. Turning back to Mahe, 'Vitora may have wanted a day to herself, and she'll be back,' she suggested.

'She takes in a *bakul*, a sarong, sandals, a head-veil, other things, her bracelets,' Mahe pointed out.

'Hm. A change of clothes, trinkets in a basket.

How do you know what she took?'

'Her mother searches, knows what is gone.'

'Ah.' Rhoda added to Fern, 'Seems our Grant has to be in on this. Even if he hasn't kidnapped Vitora, she's his headache. I'll ring him to come over. Meanwhile, will you ask young Fatimah why she's emptying her sand-bucket over Ahmad's head, and tell her to stop?'

Fern willingly busied herself with the children in order to avoid facing Grant when he came. He joined Rhoda and Mahe at Rhoda's screened desk, and some time later went out to his car with Mahe, while Rhoda came over to Fern, to tell her,

'We've wrung some kind of clue out of Mahe, whom you'll drop at her mother-in-law's on your way——'

'On *our* way?'

'Yes. Up-country for several miles. Grant wants a woman along with him, as witness, chaperon, or whatever. But he'll tell you what we've learned from Mahe as you go. So hurry, will you? He's waiting for you, and time is important.'

'Yes, but—Well, look, he's satisfied you, has he, that he hasn't had anything to do with all this?' Fern puzzled.

Rhoda confirmed, 'Not a thing. Nonplussed as we are, I swear.' Shepherding Fern towards the door, she added drily, 'Matter of interest—I don't go much on intuition, but I have a hunch he's satisfied me about more than "all this".'

'What do you mean—more than?'

Rhoda shook her head. 'Leave it to you. I could be wrong—possibly am. But listen to the story we

got from Mahe—how he tells it, and judge for
yourself.'

Bewilderedly irritable at these veiled hints,
'Why, how will he tell it?' Fern demanded.

'I *think*, as if it were as much news to him as to
us. Which, in the circumstances, is odd,' said
Rhoda.

Mahe was nervously silent in the back seat of
the car while Grant briefed Fern on their present
errand.

'Seems that some time back Vitora was forbidden an engagement to a local boy by her parents.
Name of Husain Dhar, a woodcarver and taxider-
mist who lives by selling his work, mostly to tour-
ists, in Port Dauphin and Beau Piton markets.
He's an artist at his job and got by pretty well,
though not well enough for the Sulongs, who
broke up the affair. Mahe doesn't know whether
Vitora and Husain met secretly after the split.
Selim, Mahe's husband, told her the break was
final and Vitora had got over it. But now Mahe
suggests she may have run away to the Dhar home
to join him. Mahe doesn't think it likely; the boy
hasn't been around for some time, but that's
where we are heading, just in case.'

They had reached the Sulongs' cottage and
Grant went in with her, leaving Fern no longer
puzzled by Rhoda's cryptic advice to note how he
had reported the details of Vitora's broken
romance. For he could have been talking of a total
stranger, or at best, of a girl he knew only by
having employed her! The conundrum of his detachment from the story hadn't escaped Rhoda,
who had guessed it wouldn't escape herself,

thought Fern in mounting perplexity.

For Vitora had claimed him as the father of her coming child, and how was it possible, in the various rendezvous she must have kept with him, that he hadn't learned more about her than he appeared to know now? Wasn't it likely that Vitora, fallen victim to his charm, would have chattered to him about herself; even confided to him that in falling for him, she had put behind her an earlier romance? Surely——?

Fern's thought raced on. Under pressure Vitora had confessed Grant had seduced her. He hadn't publicly denied it. It was generally supposed that he was supporting her during her pregnancy; he hadn't denied this either. *And yet*—if Rhoda's intuition and Fern's own ears hadn't deceived them, he didn't even know the girl by much more than her name!

Which made him either a consummate actor or Vitora's dupe. It wasn't even a case of her word against his, for he had given no one the satisfaction of a yea or a nay. There had been a time, Fern thought with an ache at her heart, when as his wife she would have had the right to challenge him for the truth. Dared she now—with no rights over him, not even the courtesy of sharing his name?

He was there again, taking his seat beside her, starting up.

'No co-operation there,' he said of Vitora's parents. 'Wouldn't hear of the chance she might have gone to the Dhars'. "All over, that. Finished long time ago," they said.'

'Weren't they worried? Had they anything else

to suggest?' Fern asked.

'Worried for themselves, perhaps. For what her disappearance might do to their standing with whatever is the Maraccan parallel for "the Joneses".'

Fern thought she saw an opening. 'Though it could be supposed Vitora's pregnancy outside marriage wouldn't have been too good for that.'

The opening closed. 'You'd think not,' Grant agreed coolly, then went on, 'Just as well I brought you along. Mrs Sulong would have done as well, if she'd been willing. But perhaps Rhoda told you that these Dhars might be difficult? If Vitora is there or they know where she is, they could be sticky about letting a man see her alone or wanting to take her back with him. Hence, you as chaperon.'

'I see,' said Fern. This was all in the same strange vein—as if he hadn't met the Sulongs before, as if, even to Vitora, he would be merely 'a man', instead of her guilty lover. This made no sense! *Nothing* made sense. Desperately Fern tried to frame her question. But Grant was calculating times and distances aloud, saying, 'If Vitora is on foot we might come up with her. She had a good start, but she can hardly have made this distance yet.'

'Have we much farther to go?' Fern asked.

'Not too far now. Mahe says it's the first cottage we come to in the next hamlet after the Buddhist monastery, and there *that* is now.' Grant pointed off the road across a low wall bounding an estate of lawns and flower beds surrounding the red and gold gilded buildings grouped about a domed

temple, the roof of which also glinted red and gold
in the sun. In the foreground there was a many-
arched bridge over water, reminding Fern of the
traditional willow-pattern design, and though
there were people about—shaven-headed men,
mostly alone, and gardeners working on the
beds—the whole place had an air of infinite silence
and peace. As Grant slowed the car for Fern to
take in the scene, a young man walking near the
boundary wall saluted them silently with fingertips joined beneath his chin, and Grant bowed in
return before he drove on.

'Was he a priest?' Fern asked him.

Grant shook his head. 'Much too young, I'd
say. Probably an ordinary young layman, doing
the tour of duty as a monk which all Buddhist
males have to do. It's not unlike the European
military service, except that it is not enforceable;
only a matter of honour to serve in the monastery
for a minimum of, I think, five months or any
time longer they choose, and they can do it before
or after they marry, whichever they prefer.' Grant
added drily to that, 'As they're forbidden to touch
a woman during the period of their service, it
must be quite a test of character for the oversexed,
mustn't it?'

There again might have been an opening, but
they were in sight now of the next huddle of
houses and Fern's question still went unasked.
Grant drew up at the first house they came to.
The woman who opened the door to them was
walnut-dark of skin and more lined than her
probable age should have made her. She did not
invite them in to the shadowed room behind her

and she listened impassively as Grant explained their errand in English. Then she made to close the door upon them.

Grant kept his foot in it and put a question in patois. She shook her head and with a 'She hasn't understood a word,' to Fern, he repeated his questions to the woman in an easy command of the island language which Fern had no idea he had. Herself, she understood a little, but not much, of what was being said. But when Grant finally allowed the door to close on them, she sensed he had had no success. They went back to the car. 'What?' she asked as they got in.

'Back to square one. Vitora isn't there, hasn't been there, wouldn't be expected. Neither Mrs Dhar nor her husband have seen her since the Sulongs forbade her engagement to Husain. Mrs D. is very bitter about that. And Husain isn't at home either.'

'Not? But they must know where *he* is, surely?'

'They do. He's doing his service—has been doing it for some time—at the monastery we passed just below.'

'Oh dear,' Fern sighed. 'So Vitora can't have joined him?'

'In a celibate monastery? Hardly. No, this is a dead line. Her family will have to think again, if she doesn't send them news of herself or turn up again at home.'

'Do you suppose she could have tried to leave the island by some means?' Fern debated.

'She would have needed money.'

'Well, Mahe says she took some with her, they don't know how much. *Could* she have had enough for an air ticket or a boat passage any-where?'

Grant's shrug expressed his ignorance. 'How should I know how much she could have had?'

'But don't you? Shouldn't you have an idea?' With the questions Fern had reached the limit of her patience with his utter detachment from the trouble on their hands. He had given his time and the use of his car, but had apparently no humane concern at all over whatever had driven Vitora Sulong to flight. For him, it seemed, she had little more than nuisance value—a girl he must have held in his arms ... beguiled into lovemaking. Fern shuddered away from that image, but now that she had her opening she was going to use it——

'*Oughtn't* you to know how much money Vitora had with her?' she pressed again. 'Hadn't you been sending her regular——' But her voice trailed to frustrated silence as she saw that she hadn't Grant's attention. They were passing the monas tery's bounds again on their return road, had almost reached its tall entrance gates, and Grant, pointing at a figure seated in the angle between wall and gate, was exclaiming, 'Vitora! What d'you know?'

He drew up slowly beside her, but already she was on her feet, looking about her like a hunted animal, ready to run. But Grant, out of the car, had her by the elbow, and Fern, scrambling out too, was at her other side. 'We've been looking for you, Vitora,' Fern said. 'May Sahib Grant drive you home?'

'No. No!' Vitora struggled to free herself from

Grant's firm hold. 'I wait for Husain Dhar. I must see him! He is husband, I am wife——'

'You are——?' Fern gasped her surprise and glanced quickly at Grant to note his reaction. But his expression was unreadable as he asked, 'Even so, can you hope to see Husain while he does his service?'

'No. I am woman—they will not allow. But when he comes in the gardens I shall call and he will answer me.'

'Even though to answer you would be to break his vows?' Grant questioned. 'Does he come into the gardens every day?'

'While he walks at his prayer time. But not when he goes out into the market-places with the begging-bowl. On some days he does that.'

'So that you might wait here until nightfall without seeing him? What then?'

'I find good woman in village who will give me shelter.'

'Do you know such a woman?'

Vitora admitted with a shaken head that she did not. 'But I shall find, and tomorrow I shall watch again for Husain, if not today.'

'And meanwhile you are going to get very wet.' Grant glanced up at the storm-clouds which had gathered up from the south, and from which coin-sized raindrops were already splattering the dust of the road. He said to Fern, 'Persuade her back to the car if you can. Obviously we must get her home, but first I'd like to learn more about this marriage she claims. The monastery might agree to remit or postpone the rest of Husain's service until after the child is born, if it's true that they're married.'

Fern stared at him. 'But don't *you* know whether she's married or not?' she demanded.

To which he retorted as before, 'Why should I?' adding astoundingly as he swung away towards the car, 'I'm no more in the child's confidence than you are!'

Fern had to be glad she had the now teeming rain as her ally in getting Vitora to the car. But as soon as the girl realised she was to be confined in it with them, she struggled again.

'No—I cannot!' she wailed. 'With you, Mem, not with Sahib Wilder. He will not let me go. He will beat me for what I do to him—*No!*'

Fern said, 'Sahib Wilder is not angry with you. And he will not beat you, because I won't let him.' Bundling Vitora into the back seat, she got in beside her, wrapped her own raincoat round her shivering figure, and Grant turned about in his own seat to face them.

He left the first questions to Fern, who said gently, 'Tell us, won't you, why you left home today to try to see and speak to Husain?'

Silence. Then, slowly, 'I wake in the night to know I do wrong. Every night I wake so. But today I know I must tell Husain that I do it for him, for us. For if I do not do this wrong thing, they will never let us meet or love or live happily like—Mahe and Selim. And so I do it, and must tell Husain why.'

Fern looked at Grant for enlightenment, which did not come. '*Who* will not let you love Husain?' she asked Vitora.

'My father and mother—who else?'

'But you married Husain? When?'

Vitora counted back in months. 'Four, five—but they do not know. No one in our *kampong* knows. Not Husain's mother and father. We go to a far village where Husain has friends, and they witness our marriage, making it true. And we meet and love when we can. But then Husain, who is a good Buddhist, says he must do his monk service. I am sad, but he goes, and I know he will come back.'

'When did he go?'

This time Vitora was vague about the date. 'It was before I knew I was—*so*,' she gestured towards her waistline—'and then I knew I could not tell.'

'Why not?' It was Grant who put the question.

'Because they would be more angry that I meet with Husain and marry with him. But when the doctor tell me I am so, then I think I must tell about Husain.'

'But you didn't, did you?'

Vitora hung her head. 'No, I—I did not have to say about Husain when this other Mem tell me I need not, and she will give me much money if I tell doctor and all that it is—it is——' she looked up pitifully at Grant '—it is you, Sahib Wilder, who——'

Fern's heart gave a great leap of triumph and relief and felt she could have told Grant who had bribed Vitora if he hadn't already been asking her a little wearily, 'And this Mem, who was she?'

'M—Mem Logan.'

'And has she kept her promise to give you money?'

'She send it each week by the mailman.'

'You take it and keep it, and your people think it comes from me?'

A nod. 'I keep it for Husain. For when they must know that we marry and have child, he will have money to show them; they will know he is worthy man, and they will forgive.'

'H'm, nothing like hard cash to change attitudes,' Grant commented to no one in particular, adding to Vitora, 'You knew it was wrong to do as Mem Logan asked?'

'Yes. At first I thought—you so great, Sahib, no one would judge you—but then I wake in the night and know that I must tell Husain and——'

'Yes, so you've said,' Grant cut her short and spoke to Fern. 'And so we take her home, and what do we tell "them"?'

'Why, surely all she's told us?'

'I don't know. Do you see any pressing need?'

'But of course we must,' Fern protested. 'Your name——!'

'Forget my name,' he ordered crisply. Turning front again, he switched on and let the engine idle while he seemed to be thinking aloud.

'Let's see—Vitora decided on a day out; to take a long walk——'

'I get lift in bullock-cart,' Vitora put in helpfully.

'Which explains why you got as far as you did in the time. Anyway, we catch you up. You're tired and you agree to come back with us. You say nothing at all about trying to see Husain.

Leave that to me. You do not *speak* of Husain, you understand? Today all you did was to go out alone; yesterday you were at home, waiting for your baby, tomorrow you will do the same, and when the mailman brings you more money from Mem Logan, you will take it and put it in the sock you are saving for Husain. You can do this, you think?'

Fern, listening to this inexplicable counsel, felt there could be nothing to choose between Vitora's blank bewilderment and her own. But Vitora rallied first. She said almost happily, 'I tell them nothing—Selim, Mahe, all—and I keep money and take more money and wait for Husain to finish service—so?'

'So,' Grant agreed. 'Good luck.'

They dropped Vitora at her home and watched her go in. Fern, with all she had to say to Grant, and to ask him, and to argue, could find nothing less banal as comment than, 'She's going to have to explain away that basket of overnight things she took with her.'

To which Grant replied drily, 'She's such a willing little liar that I doubt she'll have much difficulty about that.'

'You're abetting her in her lies,' Fern accused.

'Yes, why not? I may be able to pull some strings in the matter of Husain Dhar's service, but why shouldn't the lady Logan be allowed to go on doling out the cash grant for a few weeks or months more?'

'You *must* know why she can't!' Fern declared furiously. 'You've *got* to clear your name of this scandal you know is being talked about you!'

'In my own time.'

'As if you could choose the time to kill something that's been common rumour for weeks! Not that rumour doesn't sometimes get it right. You gave me a roasting for tattling to Father about the Logans, but now it's proved they're working against you, you still won't do anything about it!'

'Your gossiping to Sir Manfred was premature and impertinent. Now I prefer the Logans should dig their graves for a while longer and deeper.'

'But this—about your having seduced Vitora— is personal to you, utterly damaging, ruinous——' Fern battled.

'A good deal more damaging to my self-esteem if it were true. I know it isn't, and that's all that matters for the moment.' Grant turned to look at her. 'Anyway, why are you working yourself into a passion about it? What is my allegedly grimy reputation to you?'

Fern bit her lip. 'It—matters to me,' she said, and waited. Waited for him to read into the admission the hidden feelings of love and loyalty it hadn't expressed. But when he said nothing in reply, she had a sudden savage urge to hit back. 'I'm surprised that you shouldn't care about Rose de Mille's reaction to your grimy reputation,' she said tartly. 'She must have heard the talk and can't be too pleased.'

Grant's reply was a short laugh. 'Rose is a realist and woman-of-the-world to a degree,' he said. 'If she has any reaction to my philandering with Vitora, she's probably pleased with such evidence of my virility.'

'As if you haven't given her enough evidence of

that already! Why should she need more?' Wearying of the argument which she knew she couldn't win, Fern made a last attempt at defiance.

'You needn't think I'm going to tell Rhoda all these lies about Vitora's having merely gone for a walk,' she declared. 'She's my best friend here, my only real friend, and I want no part in deceiving her.'

Grant said grimly, 'You'll leave *me* to tell her all I consider anyone on the camp need know at present.' He paused. 'That's an order. Understood?'

She left him to make of her closed expression and silence whatever he would.

CHAPTER NINE

FACED with the dilemma of how much to tell Rhoda without disobeying Grant, Fern compromised by agreeing there was no doubt that he and Vitora were the strangers they could not possibly be if he had indeed seduced her.

'Easy—I guessed as much,' Rhoda confirmed with satisfaction. 'It means the girl lied in naming him, and there's only one reason for that.'

'Yes,' said Fern flatly.

'Shielding her lover, whoever he is,' Rhoda claimed, getting it half right and, to Fern's relief, seeming disposed to leave it there, after adding a dry opinion that Grant, having ignored the gossip so far, could be trusted to see it into the ground in the end.

But could he? Fern wondered, when he had made no move against the Logans at the end of a week. What was he waiting for? While he allowed them to dig their grave, with every day that passed their subversion was digging his. And if he left his exposure of them until he was about to leave Maracca for Norway, they could thwart him by claiming that as a failed manager and an undesirable philanderer, he was being driven out, and they would be believed.

Fern's own plans veered like a weather-vane in

a punishing wind. She would wait to see it all happen—No, she could not bear to see him go. She must wait for a time in fairness to Rhoda— But if she didn't consider Rhoda, she could go now, why not——? Thoughts which had argued one way yesterday were reasoning differently today. But one persisted and became paramount. Before she left Maracca or Grant did, she had to know whether Rose de Mille would be going with him or would follow him. *Had* to know . . .

Apart from Grant or Rose, the one person who might tell her was Sophie Dean, Rose's accompanist. Sophie, who acted also as Rose's dresser, secretary and public relations officer, led a somewhat hunted existence, and was usually only to be caught when she was snatching a hasty buffet meal in the Meurice's coffee-shop. She and Fern knew each other by sight and a few exchanged words, and Fern, feeling all the guilt of an amateur spy, followed Sophie from the counter one lunchtime, and invited herself to share her table.

'Of course. Do,' Sophie agreed, beginning on the contents of her tray with a speed which suggested bears were snapping at her heels. Fern saw there was going to be little time for delicate manoeuvring into the subject of Rose's plans; she would have to settle for whatever Sophie might know of Rose's future public movements, and after a few conversational nothings, she put the blunt question, 'At the end of your season here, where do you go next?'

About to launch herself upon her creme caramel, 'Where do *I* go?' Sophie enquired.

'You and Madame de Mille, I meant.'

'Not the same thing this time,' Sophie pointed out. '*I* am going home for a long rest. Rose is——'

'You're leaving her?' Fern asked in surprise.

'Because I've been with her, man and boy, for seven years, and I've had it. What she needs isn't one female slave but a retinue of us, and I'm through,' Sophie returned crisply.

'So that, when she leaves here, she'll be going alone?'

'Uhuh. To Oslo for the winter season. Not that she will take long to replace me; a job with la de Mille has glamour to it——' Sophie gulped coffee, used her napkin and picked up her bag. 'Got to run now. *Always* running. So long. See you around——' she called over her shoulder to Fern, and was gone.

Oslo. Norway. Fern hadn't had to pump for the information; Sophie had volunteered it without a clue to the knell it had sounded for Fern. Grant was going to Norway. Rose de Mille was going to Norway. Fern felt hollow inside with an emptiness that had nothing to do with hunger. It was a desolate void of despair.

Since all she had got from Sophie was no more than everyone soon knew, she need not have bothered. For the Meurice was heralding the end of Maracca's exclusive winter season with the announcement of a Gala Dinner and Ball at which Rose de Mille would be its guest of honour, 'prior to her departure north to Norway for her next engagement'.

As no one yet knew of Grant's coming 'departure north' no one was able to make gossip out of the coincidence. But there was plenty more about which to speculate—for instance, how far the Wilder–de Mille affair had advanced towards marriage—if at all, since the Wilder–Vitora Sulong scandal had hit the headlines, or whether, if Rose chose to overlook that affair, she would accept Grant and not go to Norway at all. But in face of the trouble and unrest in the oil camp, how long could Grant hold down his job as manager there? Surely, unless he had some underhand influence with Sir Manfred, Opal would consider replacing him soon?

And how the Logans must enjoy fostering *that* one, thought Fern, seething with frustrated indignation for Grant when he still continued to ignore the explosive situation as if it didn't exist.

When the Meurice confirmed the date of its Gala she was reminded of the first she had attended there, the night when Grant had partnered her, when she had seen her wedding ring flung carelessly into a drawer, and when later Grant had teased her desire for him, claiming he had meant to tantalise her and no more. Since then, while Ben was courting her, he had been her willing escort to parties. But now there was no one whose invitation to this Gala she would accept. Its advertised purpose of fêting Rose was enough to keep her away, as she was to tell Grant with some acidity when to her utter surprise he rang up to suggest that she go with him.

'You have to be joking,' she told him. 'I'm not going to be there.'

'Not? Why not? Haven't you read the posters? It's to be a Maraccan Occasion which Nobody can Afford to Miss,' he quoted the hotel's publicity in all its persuasive capital letters.

'A Rose de Mille Occasion, which you can hardly expect me to support!' Fern snapped back.

'Tch, tch! Jealousy rearing its ugly head? For shame! You know Rose, as I do, for a beautiful, talented, purposeful woman. But you can't take it, can you? You aren't generous enough to give her the send-off she deserves and has earned, is that it?'

Stung, Fern retorted, 'Perhaps I'm not as generous as you'd like, because I can't see *her* send-off and *your* leaving for much the same destination as the coincidence you'd have me believe it to be!'

In the pause which followed she could envisage his shrug of indifference. Then, 'Sorry, but coincidence all the same. Rose makes her own contracts with her agents, and Opal didn't consult me before deciding to offer me Norway next,' he reminded her blandly.

'But how fortunate for you that they did!' she jeered.

'As you say—could make for a happy fall-out all round,' he agreed.

'I can hardly wait,' she murmured, hoping the sarcasm would get through to him.

'Then don't. Be there with me to witness Rose's Benefit Night in all its glorious Technicolor,' he urged. 'Will you come?'

'And tag along as the third in a crowd of you, Rose de Mille and myself, I suppose?' she evaded, suddenly and perversely wishing she had said yes, lest he shouldn't ask her again.

Grant didn't ask her again. He scoffed, 'Nothing of the sort. Rose will be the lion of the evening, the toast of all the V.I.P.s of the island, with the rest of us mere onlookers,' and assumed he had Fern's agreement by adding, 'That's a date, then. Thank you,' as if he had known all along she would not refuse him.

When she dressed for the Gala evening she did so in a simple black dress, determined that Grant shouldn't suppose she was trying to outdo Rose in glamour, which she acknowledged she never could. As she dressed she wondered how and when Grant would ask her to release him from their travesty of a marriage. Perhaps even tonight—who knew?

The hotel's publicity had certainly paid off. The foyer was crowded, the bars were impassable, the dining-room glittered like a magician's cave and Rose was 'receiving' the patrons as graciously as if she were a private hostess and they her guests. At dinner she was flanked at the top table by the Mayor and his deputy, as remote from the herd as if she were royalty. After dinner she did not dance when other people did, and she was asked to sing only once. She chose a short cycle of peasant songs from the Auvergne, bowing out to a clamour of applause and disappearing herself shortly afterwards at midnight. There was nothing Rose did not know about giving her public (and possibly her men?) just enough to keep them hungry, thought Fern jealously, though forced to admit Rose was managing her leavetaking of Maracca superbly.

With her departure the party began to break up. In the foyer when Fern excused herself to Grant to fetch her wrap, he said, 'You're not going back just yet. You're coming up to the apartment with me.'

She suppressed a shiver of apprehension. Had she wondered aright, and this was the showdown they would have to have if he wanted his freedom to marry Rose? 'Why?' she asked.

'Because I say so.'

She hung back. 'That's no reason.'

'It's a good enough substitute. Come along.'

The elevator hummed upward. Grant unlocked the door of his suite on to the living-room, which was in darkness. Someone who was sitting in a chair facing the window turned about as Grant switched on a light, and with a choked cry of surprise Fern darted forward.

'Father!' She ran into Sir Manfred's arms, turning back to accuse Grant, 'You *knew*, and you didn't tell me!' Back again to Sir Manfred, 'When? How did you come? Oh, you don't know how glad I am to see you!' She was very near to tears.

He smoothed her hair, its vibrant electricity lifting against his palm. 'By the afternoon plane from Durban. Grant has kept me under wraps because he didn't want you to miss the Gala thing below,' he told her.

'You mean *he* didn't want to miss it!'

Grant came over from pouring drinks. 'Same thing,' he said. 'I didn't want to be stood up for a dinner partner at the last moment——' He broke off as the house telephone rang. 'Excuse me.'

They listened as he answered his caller, 'Yes. No. No trouble at all. In fact, I find myself slightly *de trop* at the moment. I'll explain when I see you. I'll be right along.' He replaced the receiver and Fern, not needing to ask, said sourly, 'That was Rose de Mille.'

'Yes.'

'At this hour? She could have seen you at any time of this evening!'

'Technically we shall be chaperoned by Sophie, even if she's in bed and asleep,' he said imperturbably, and nodded to Sir Manfred. 'I'll be back.'

'He's in *love* with her,' Fern burst out when the door had closed behind him. 'He just makes use of me as he did tonight. You heard him admit it. And she only has to beckon him and he runs— you heard that too.'

'Also heard you trotting out a corny line in jealousy. You did stop short of calling Rose de Mille "that woman", but I imagine, only just,' Sir Manfred said quietly.

'I am *not* jealous,' she denied. 'That's—all over. What I do resent is his expecting me to be complaisant about it, that's all. He doesn't *mind* my knowing he sees her and thinks she's wonderful. He—he flaunts her at me, that's what. Did you know, for instance, that she's going to Oslo for her next engagement, when he is going to Norway on the job? And what do you bet,' she finished wildly, 'that she's called him now to discuss their travel plans?'

Sir Manfred said, 'I should very much doubt that. Grant has far too many problems to tie up here before he leaves. As you should know.'

'Oh, I do. I didn't really mean that about travel plans. I shouldn't think even Grant would insult me by actually travelling *with* her.' Wearily Fern swept a hand under the fall of her hair. 'Is that why you've come out again, Father? To iron out his problems for him?'

'To watch him solve them for himself.'

'You know of the lies Freda Logan invented to accuse him of seducing one of his office girls?'

'Yes, I've been posted on that.'

'He was angry with me for writing to you that the Logans were working against him.'

'He rightly resented your jumping the gun on rumour while he had no proof.'

'But since he's had it, he's done nothing about it!'

'He'll be doing it from now on. And hasn't he told you that though he's pulled some strings to get that young husband's release from his monk service, his pregnant wife won't hear of it?'

'He doesn't tell me anything he needn't,' Fern murmured.

'No—well, the girl told Grant virtuously that her husband must do his time for Buddha—motivated by piety or by knowing that as soon as the truth of their marriage is out, the money from the Logans will stop, Grant doesn't know,' Sir Manfred chuckled.

Fern had to laugh too. 'Grant said he didn't see why Freda should be let off that hook too soon.'

'No, though the girl will have to settle for reputation instead of cash when Austin Logan will be invited to resign, and they'll leave the island soon.'

'Before Grant goes?'

'Before anyone on the camp, except you, Grant and me, know that we've made him the offer of the Norway site—and no one is to know while Grant is still here.'

'Why is that?'

'Because,' said Sir Manfred, 'he says his best chance of repairing the damage the Logans have done is enough continuity to give the men back their sense of security, and I'm prepared to go along with that until they've gained it and can take a new management in their stride when the time comes for it.'

'When he goes to Norway, leaving this job unfinished!'

'Unfortunately, yes. But Norway is new and right in his field, and when it came up we had to make him the offer. And I daresay you realise the personal issues which may have influenced his decision?'

'You don't have to edge your way round words, Father!' Fern's tone was bitter. '*I'm* one of the personal affairs Grant has to wind up and parcel away before he leaves, aren't I?'

'If nothing has changed between you since I saw you last, you don't give him much choice, do you?' said Sir Manfred.

Fern accused, 'Now you're judging me, as you did when you let Grant persuade you to abandon me here! You both thought I was so good-for-nothing that I'd be dependent on him and give in. But I got myself a job, and you are right—nothing *has* changed for us. We are exactly where we were when you tricked me into coming here and he publicly disowned me.'

'Though you seem to have weathered some crises and are still here,' Sir Manfred pointed out. 'There's been Grant's involvement with Rose de Mille and the scandal over the Buddhist girl. While you didn't know the truth of that, it must have taken some dogged courage to hang on, when there was nothing to stop your taking the first flight home. Why didn't you?'

'I—like it here.'

'And when Grant goes?'

Fern was silent. She was looking at a Maracca where no Grant would be, and it was a prospect she didn't want to contemplate.

'I suppose I shall come home when you go. I shall have to warn Rhoda Camell that I may.'

'I'll be glad to have you, love. You know that,' her father assured her warmly. 'There's no possible chance of your changing your mind about Norway?'

'Changing my mind? I wasn't consulted about Norway—just told he'd been given the offer, that's all!' she exploded.

Sir Manfred spread despairing hands. 'He evidently wasn't wasting his breath to ask you to join him. You know, daughter mine, there's a limit to the humiliation a man will take at the hands of a woman.'

'And haven't I taken enough at his?'

'Enough, obviously, on both sides for it to be deadlock between you. As you say, this is where we came in.' Sir Manfred watched her stand and turn towards the door. 'Aren't you waiting for Grant to see you home?'

'Coming straight to me from——? What do you think?' she scorned.

'Go ahead, call her "that woman" if it helps!'

'It doesn't. Where are you staying, Father?'

'I have a room here until the yacht comes out from England for me—for us, if that's the way you want it. Come along, I'll see you home by taxi.'

'Thank you. And—that is the way I want it,' she lied, biting on the words.

'Only by your own choice, love,' Sir Manfred countered mildly. On Grant's side as always. Never on hers. That wasn't fair thinking, she knew. But it helped her bruised self-pity to believe it.

Whatever was the expertise and diplomacy Grant used on the problems which the discredited Logans left behind them, it worked. Resentful as she was of him, Fern had to admire his dedication to a task, the long-term results of which he had chosen not to stay to see. But that was Grant, she knew—thorough-paced in everything, even his uncompromising rejection of her.

The matter of his leaving remained a well kept secret, and she still had no indication of his intentions towards Rose when Rose departed on the day before *Calypso* sailed in and Sir Manfred transferred to his stateroom in it, where Fern, visiting him there, was torn between seeing the yacht as a refuge and a prison cage. Though they had met briefly, there had been no clash with Grant since her father's arrival, when he had rung her up the next day to ask why she had not waited for him to take her home to the creche.

Hackles ready to stand on end, 'How was I to know you weren't going to spend the rest of the night where you were?' she had demanded, and hadn't been disarmed by his careless laugh.

'Dragooned by Sophie in the next room? If I'd contemplated an all-night session with Rose, I'd have fixed a less public rendezvous. But if you recall, *she* had invited *me*,' he had reminded her.

'What did she want of you?'

'To be congratulated on the success of her evening. Like all artists, she thrives on appreciation. Besides, wasn't I giving you the chance of a cosy get-together with your father?'

'Which I had, thank you.'

'Reporting on the non-progress of our singular and delicate negotiations? And then fleeing the coop to show me where I got off?'

'Refusing to await your pleasure in collecting

me. *When* you were ready to leave th— your girl-friend.'

'Though I bet you had a struggle between standing me up and waiting to administer a curtain lecture?' he had taunted and had hung up without waiting for her reply.

Now she found herself in a vacuum. Working as usual at the creche, managing to see her father on most days, though avoiding Grant, she was aware only of waiting for all this to end when Maracca and its magic would become an episode in her past and there would be no Grant in her future.

She had told Rhoda she would be leaving in *Calypso* with Sir Manfred, and was grateful that Rhoda didn't make a grievance of it.

'Consider I was lucky to keep you after Ben Croftus went to Brazil,' Rhoda commented. 'I knew it wasn't a permanency for you, of course, but we've fitted pretty well, haven't we?'

'You've helped me to fit, and taught me a lot,' Fern told her warmly.

'Well, don't forget it all before you have babies of your own,' advised Rhoda. She thought for a moment, then, 'I daresay Mahe will come back to fill the gap you'll leave. Some competition there,' she added dryly. 'Sister-in-law Vitora with a baby well on its way, and Mahe not even pregnant yet. M'm, yes, I think Mahe will come running if I ask her.'

Fern supposed there would be a day when she would hear that Sir Manfred was ready to sail, probably within twenty-four hours. But there was to be no such day. When she arrived at *Calypso* one late afternoon, she found him directing his steward in the packing of a valise while using the telephone himself. Listening to his caller, he made a silencing gesture at Fern and presently replaced the receiver.

'That was England—Scotland, rather,' he told Fern. 'One of our rigs off the west coast has come adrift and is in danger of sinking. Reception is poor and the details aren't clear. But I shall have to get over. I can't wait to sail. I'm catching the evening flight over to Durban, and I shall connect from there.'

Fern gasped. 'Oh, Father, how awful!' This had happened to the offshore rigs of other oil consortiums, she knew, though tragedy had never yet hit Opal. She made a quick decision. 'I'll come with you, Father. If there isn't time for me to collect my things, I'll come as I am.'

Sir Manfred dealt shortly with that offer. 'There isn't time, and you are not coming,' he ruled. 'I'm going straight up to the site, where there'll be nothing you can do to help. No, love, you'll stay here for the time being, and you can do something for me when I've gone. Grant had to fly to the mainland yesterday, due back this evening. I'll leave behind a message for him when he flies in, but I want you to find him and give him any further news which may turn up tonight. You'll do that?'

'Yes. I'll ring the airport to find out when he——' She broke off as the telephone rang and her father leapt to it.

'Yes?' he barked into the mouthpiece, then questioned 'Two?' listened against for a time and hung up.

'Two lives feared lost, one a married man,' he reported to Fern, then fastened his case and sent the steward to confirm that his cab was waiting. When she went down with him to the quay he was almost too preoccupied to bid her goodbye. He kissed her absently, said, 'Put Grant in the picture, and go to him if you need anything.' Then he was gone and she was alone.

She went back on board. Without being asked the steward brought tea and Fern drank it with eager thirst, as if it were a drug she craved.

For on her mind and drumming in her ears were the blunt words of that latest bulletin from the rig. *Two feared lost, one a.married man*—the impersonal brevity of a news item to be met with in the Press almost every day in this or that connection. *Two lives*, and behind one of them at least, a woman who had been a wife. The cruel parallel she drew from it almost took her breath away.

One day there might be just the same laconic notice—about Grant. Grant in danger; Grant 'feared lost' in just such a disaster as this, and she not near him, perhaps not even belonging to him any more, lost to him and he to her, because she hadn't been willing to follow him where he had to lead; had refused to dip her silly pride an inch in order to keep him, to—to *deserve* him.

Her self-reproach was like a physical pain, an ache which tore at her whole being. It was too late now. Grant was committed to a future with Rose, and when he had told her about Norway he hadn't even asked her to go with him. And yet she was still his wife, wasn't she? If there were any pity in him, any last remnant of the love they had shared, mightn't he listen if she told him how wrong she had been, how criminally reckless of losing him, when in truth he was all she wanted in the world?

In an agony of bemused thought she remained curled on the window seat of her father's cabin for a long time. At last she bestirred herself to ring Rhoda to tell her what had happened and that she might be late back if Grant's plane were delayed. Then she called the airport, to hear that the flight had in fact landed early and the passengers had dispersed, and yes—in answer to her query—Sahib Wilder had been among them, had collected his car from the park and had driven away. So much for a small enough airport to know most of its patrons by name or sight, thought Fern, headily grateful that he had arrived.

She gave him time to drive to the camp club, but was told he had not gone there. Next she tried his apartment at the Meurice. His telephone was not answered. Nor, though she had him paged, was he in the hotel.

But when another call to each brought no result, her patience gave out. She had to do something, be on the move. She telephoned for Cristo, the taxi-driver she and Sir Manfred used, and was waiting for him on the quay when he came.

The Meurice first, as that was nearer than the camp. She would leave a message there, and then drive out to the club. It was not until Cristo was halfway into the city from the docks that another possibility dawned. Why hadn't it occurred to her that even if Sir Manfred's message hadn't reached him, after a business trip to the mainland, he would almost certainly go to report to his Chief in *Calypso*?

She stopped Cristo and ordered their turn-about. At the docks again—yes, there was Grant's car on the quay. With her heart seeming to beat almost in her throat she ran up the gangway, to be met by the deck steward telling her, 'Mr Wilder asked to be shown into Sir Manfred's stateroom. He is waiting for you there.'

Grant was at Sir Manfred's desk when Fern went in. Breathless from her hurry, she panted, 'Grant, you got Father's message?' and nodding, he came forward.

'About the Scottish rig? Yes. He said you would be here and might have some later news.'

She shook her head. 'There's been no more. But you couldn't have come here straight from the airport, or you'd have arrived before I left to find you—at your apartment, I supposed, or out at Le Corsair.'

'I did call in at the apartment to fetch something and left again at once, which is how you missed me.'

'Oh, I see.' There was an awkward pause while she was casting about in her mind for an opening for what she had planned to tell him, however humiliating the outcome. Unable to blurt it à propos of nothing, she said, 'There were casualties on the rig—did Father say so? Probably at least two men killed. And even if there were no more, it made me think——' She checked. This was too difficult.

Grant waited, then prompted, 'Think what?'

'Well, that it could happen on any offshore rig. Any time——'

He nodded. 'Has done. Will again. Possibly with a good deal heavier toll than two.'

'But for the two! They were two *people*, and someone would have loved them. And when I thought that—that one of them might some day be you, I couldn't bear it! I wouldn't go to the Gulf with you. I wouldn't have come here if I'd known you were here. I was even ready to refuse to go to Norway with you——' She had to press a fist to her shaking lips before she could go on. When she could, 'Always supposing you'd asked me,' she finished, and had to use the same fist to brush childishly at her eyes.

Grant pulled her down to sit beside him. 'And I didn't ask you, did I?' he said.

'No. And now it's too late. I only—I just wanted you to know——'

'That you'd take on Norway now if I should ask you?'

She managed a wan smile. 'Oh, Grant, I'd come running, little fool that I've been. But now there's Rose.'

'Forget Rose for the moment. She's another story. She doesn't affect ours. Listen, little fool, and you said it, I didn't, supposing I tell you that if you want to beat it for Norway, you'll be going alone?' He seemed to be savouring the dumb incomprehension of her stare as he went on,

'Because I'm not going. I never was.'

It took seconds for that to register. Then her deep sense of betrayal accused him, 'You mean you lied to me? Father has lied to me? *Why?*'

Grant said, 'In a worthy cause, we thought. Ends justifying means and all that. Putting on a screw which might or might not work. The first one didn't.'

Slowly shocked understanding dawned. 'A screw on *me*?'

He nodded. 'When the Chief sailed away in this brig, we thought that leaving you here on your own would drive you into rejoining me sooner or later.'

'You made it impossible for me to come back to you. You wouldn't acknowledge we were married!' Fern protested.

'I wasn't going to acknowledge a wife who wouldn't live with me. However, we tried again. I kept you guessing about Rose——'

'I'm still having to guess about Rose!'

'Not any more. I was nursing along your jealousy of her, that's all. It hasn't been difficult to admire Rose aloud. She's a beautiful woman, talented, dedicated to her work, outgoing—and married.'

'*Married?*'

'To a paraplegic in a wheelchair for life, to whom she's as dedicated and devoted as she is to her singing. They live, between her engagements, in Paris, and she's there with him now before she goes to her date in Oslo. The few weeks they snatch together mean everything to them, and

she's a lioness about guarding their marriage and
his complete financial dependence on her from
publicity.'

'Her being married hasn't stopped her
from laying a lot of claim to you,' Fern
grumbled.

'You could say I encouraged her for my own
ends,' Grant admitted. 'But though she collects
men's homage as buddleia attracts butterflies in
August, she draws a very firm line across her intimacy with them, which none of them is allowed
to cross.'

'Not even you?'

'I was never tempted to explore the other side
of the line.' Grant smiled rather wryly. 'I had
other fish to fry, and I was doing my sums. Your
jealousy of Rose, plus my mythical acceptance of
the Norway project, ought to break your bone-
headed pride some time, I argued.'

'You made me suffer over Rose, and if I've been
as stubborn as all that, I've only learnt it from
you,' Fern retorted with spirit.

Grant said, 'It hasn't been pride that's been
biting me. I've only been standing by my right
to expect that when we married "for better,
for worse" meant living and loving and working
together. Wherever my job took me, you should
be willing to go, because I asked you to and
needed you, though with the difference over
the Norway bit, that I wasn't going to ask you.
You were to be driven into asking *me* to take
you. Your father and I were going to confront
you with a phoney definite date for my going,
hoping—though we should have known

better—to force you into giving in or turning me down for good.' He paused to draw a long sigh. 'Pity we went to so much trouble to wear you down, when you seem to have made it under your own steam.'

'But I haven't. I didn't,' Fern accused herself, suddenly contrite. 'I've told you, it was the news about those two men lost from the rig. If they hadn't been killed, I might still have lost you through being too proud to ask anything of you. Don't you see? If I've really got you back, I can't forget that I've bought you at the price of their two lives?'

'You must forget it, sweetheart.' He drew her to him and held back the curtain of hair which was hiding her drooped face. 'If you hadn't been ripe for coming back to me, the message of those men's deaths wouldn't have got through to you. You'd have felt pity for them, but no more. As it was, they taught you fear for me and——'

There the telephone shrilled its interruption and they both started up. Receiver at his ear, Grant signalled, 'Scotland. Another bulletin.' Then Fern was hearing only his side of the conversation.

'No. He left Maracca on the evening flight out. I'm his son-in-law, Wilder of Opal Maracca, and my wife is here with me.' Then there seemed to be some discussion as to when Sir Manfred might be expected at the other end, and then Grant was listening for some time.

When he hung up he turned to Fern. 'They hope to be able to salvage the rig, and there are no casualties at all. They'd got the count wrong;

the two missing men had reported sick earlier and weren't on board.'

She glowed. 'Oh, Grant—truly?' On the impulse of the moment of sheer relief she flung her arms round him and found herself held fast. Leaning against him, 'You can't think what it did for me to hear you call me your wife,' she whispered.

'*What* did it do for you?'

'Made me go all tingly with pleasure.'

'Only tingly? You must do better than that.' His finger tilted her chin. 'Though do you realise, madam, that here we can't suddenly emerge as a Mr and a Mrs without the formality of an engagement, however short, and a wedding ceremony to follow?'

'Oh! So we can't!' she agreed blankly. 'But how can we have another wedding? If we've never stopped being married to each other, would it even be legal?'

'I don't know. But don't look so worried, my neither-maid-nor-wife. It's all been taken care of,' he assured her.

She stared. 'What do you mean? How could it be, when you couldn't have known I was ready to beg you to take me back?'

'We could only keep our fingers crossed. Your father argued that if I really didn't count with you, you'd have cut your losses and gone back home long ago, and even I had a hunch you were protesting a shade too much about your independence of me. Just possibly you did still care. And if you should say yes to our Norway-or-else ultimatum, we had to have a plan ready to extricate us all from that one.'

'Because it was all a plant, and you weren't ever going to Norway?'

'Exactly. But as we can't carry on here without being seen to be married, we must both disappear together for long enough for Romance to have dawned for us and got us to the altar somewhere else, before we come back.'

Fern said, 'Oh!' again, and then, anxiously, 'We are coming back?'

'Of course. The offer of the Norway site was tempting, but I'd got my teeth so deeply into this job that I never really considered it.'

'Except for using it as a lever on me! But where do we disappear to when we go?'

'To England, naturally. You're already known to be going home and I go on the periodical leave that's due to me. Two months or so hence, love will have burgeoned for us and our marriage in England will be behind us and our foreseeable future here in front.' Grant's finger traced a gentle line from her temple to her chin, across her jaw and up the curve of her other cheek, as if he were committing the oval of her face to the memory of a pencil. 'Suit you, my lovely, does it?' he asked.

'Oh yes, *yes*! How soon can we go?'

'The idea was that, if the whole thing hadn't ended in deadlock, the three of us would be going back together by yacht. But now I don't know. We shall have to wait for briefing by the Chief when he can get around to it.'

'May we speak to him tomorrow when he'll have arrived at the site? And Grant, there's one thing——'

'Yes?'

'When we do come back, may I tell Rhoda the truth about us? It won't go any further on from her, for she's so laconic and taciturn that telling her anything is rather like digging a hole, shouting down it and covering it over. She'd never bother to resurrect it or even remember it for long. And she's been such a friend to me that I couldn't bear to deceive her any more than I need. Please?'

Grant nodded. 'I know. On the camp she's always had the reputation of a prize clam. So go ahead, if you feel you must.'

'And supposing I found myself with some spare time on my hands, could I sometimes go and help her with the children again?'

'What a suppliant, obedient little shrew you're turning into!' he mocked her. ' "May I?" "Can we?" Don't get too biddable, will you, or you won't be my Fern. And how much twiddle-thumb time do you suppose you'll have left from being my housekeeper and my hostess and my playmate and the only mistress of my heart—tell me?'

She giggled happily. 'There'll still be some— when you're at work.'

'As long as I have the prior claim——' Then, all the badinage gone from his tone, he was plead- ing, 'Fern, my sweet, we've waited so long. Need we waste any *more* time now? You know what I want of you—don't you?'

She knew. All the straining of his body to hers, the questing of his roving hands, the naked desire in his eyes, were telling her without need of words. And she wanted the same of him. All the pent-up sensual hungers of months and years were welling in her, turning her into a primaeval woman, savagely eager for her man.

She told him so in the hot response of her lips to his kisses and in the searching of her own hands for the touch of his vibrant, sunbronzed skin.

There was no embarrased virgin shyness between them. Everything about his body was remembered and familiar, and she sensed that he was rediscovering every curve and warmth of hers. She did not resist when he led her gently to the bed alcove where he sat beside her, caressing and smoothing, and following the contours of shoulders and breast beneath the thin silk of her dress. There was only a simple wrap-over waist tie between him and her bare flesh, and when he had mastered its knot, with a little groan of delight his lips took their toll of the slim body which the discarded silk revealed.

The rest was inevitable. Their need of each other clamoured to be assuaged in the ultimate expression of marriage; their sensuality was a surging tide which swept them inexorably to the sweet, rapturous union where desire peaked and erupted, then stilled to a deep content.

They lay for a long while in a haze of fulfilment, murmuring gratitudes, enlacing fingers, talking a little of nothing that mattered. Slowly, reluctantly, they came back to reality. Grant said, 'We'll invite ourselves to dinner here, and then I must take you home. Rhoda will want to hear the better news.'

'Yes.' Fern watched as he took something from the pocket of his shirt and reached for her left hand. 'With my body I thee worship . . .' he quoted softly, and looking down, she saw the gleam of her wedding ring clasping its proper finger.

'Oh, Grant, you brought it with you! How could you have known I was ready to give in?' she breathed.

'I went to fetch it before I came to you from the airport. I didn't know. But I was hoping,' he said.

A WORD ABOUT THE AUTHOR

When Jane Arbor is writing a book, the characters people her day—though intruding on her conscious mind only during the hours she is actually working. "For the rest of the time," she says "it's as if I were rich in children who are away at boarding school. They're temporarily out of mind, but despite the absence, still there.

"Even so," Jane continues, "I am less of a human mother than a feline mother with kittens. As soon as a manuscript is finished—as soon as the kittens are ready to make homes of their own—I forget it. Within a week, I am worrying about my next book."

People often ask this Harlequin veteran—she has been writing Romances for almost twenty-five years—if she ever portrays anyone she knows or has known, and her answer is an emphatic *no.* "But," she admits, "I do note characteristics of real people and transplant them into imagined characters with entirely different backgrounds. This I regard as legitimate poaching."

Jane Arbor has lived in the same "Anne Hathaway thatched cottage" north of the Thames River for more than thirty years. It's an enchanting spot where, above everything else, she enjoys her job—"writing books that people want to read."

Legacy of
PASSION

BY CATHERINE KAY

A love story begun long ago comes full circle…

Venice, 1819: Contessa Allegra di Rienzi, young, innocent, unhappily married. She gave her love to Lord Byron—scandalous, irresistible English poet. Their brief, tempestuous affair left her with a shattered heart, a few poignant mementos—and a daughter he never knew about.

Boston, today: Allegra Brent, modern, independent, restless. She learned the secret of her great-great-great-grandmother and journeyed to Venice to find the di Rienzi heirs. There she met the handsome, cynical, blood-stirring Conte Renaldo di Rienzi, and like her ancestor before her, recklessly, hopelessly lost her heart.

Choose from this great selection of early Harlequins—books that let you escape to the wonderful world of romance!*

ome of these book were originally published under different titles.